FAE
CAME
ON
THE
PLANE!

By
Elizabeth Watasin

A-GIRL STUDIO

CHAPTER ONE

Starships appeared in a blue sky similar to Earth's, but for the dazed chrono-arrivals processed through Again New York's immigration at Jifk spaceport, it was a blue sky 400 light years from a familiar solar system. Perhaps the elder gods who had long ago departed Old Earth to found Darqueworld in the Merope Nebula had created that blue sky, breathable atmosphere, and blue seas. The Other-beings, humans, and time travellers lucky enough to make it to the planet did not question the liveable environment. Darqueworld was where Old Earth's secret beings could begin anew.

Nico Alexikova, death-age at eighteen and fifteen years a vampire, studied her reflection in the aluminium siding of the 50s style diner, Lucy's, and straightened the narrow black tie she wore with a silk dress shirt and black cardigan. Though in her usual black stockings, that day she wore a short skirt of Black Watch tartan rather than of solid grey or black. Its dark green complemented the bright green paper wrapped around the bouquet of twelve closed red roses and four pure white Casa Blanca lilies cradled in Nico's arm. The flowers, in Nico's estimation, looked gorgeous.

It had taken some time getting used to seeing her reflection and being out in the sun without fear of burning up. But she was making great progress with both phobias, as her therapist told her, which were common afflictions for vampire chrono-immigrants.

However, as a recent arrival from the later 20th century who still needed to view the X-Files seasons she'd missed, Nico did not think she would ever become complacent with the sight of starships, lifting and landing at Jifk spaceport. She glanced up and admired a spinning vessel whirring for the stratosphere right then.

She stood behind the diner car that had been her first haven when arriving at Jifk spaceport and Again NewYork. There, she'd met a young waitress, witch, and weird matter wielder who became her lover, too. Shayla O'Fey exited Lucy's scullery door and smiled warmly. She held two mugs and sat down at the employee break table by the door, blonde hair shining in the sunlight. Despite the utilitarian cut of her pink waitress's uniform, Nico thought the outfit flattered Shayla—or perhaps it was Shayla's figure that flattered the outfit. A corsage of one lily and closed red rose was pinned above Shayla's nametag.

Nico sucked in breath, tasting Shayla's creamy peach-and-bergamot scent.

"Don't you and Mr Bear look bonnie," Shayla said, her Scots accent easy and laid back. Her hazel-eyed gaze twinkled as Nico approached, self-consciously adjusting the leather chest harness in which her tan stuffed teddy bear, Mr Bear, sat. "Ye should have a matchin' boutonniere, love."

Nico shook her head and bit her lip against a shy grin. Not only did the flowers cost her half her hotel desk clerk wage for the week, but their symbolism screamed "everlasting love" to her two lovers. Shayla, born to Darqueworld, might not take roses and lilies as such, but Heloise—tall, dark, and gorgeous Heloise Allen, a 21st century vampire who rose in the fifties—would clearly read their meaning.

"Have yer blood, love." Shayla sipped her coffee as Nico joined her at the table, laying her wrapped flowers carefully aside. Pulling up the Id she stored in a pocket behind Bear—a popular, pad-shaped personal computer devise she'd named *Dorothy* for Dorothy Gale—Nico checked the time.

Heloise's flight from New London would arrive in a little over an hour. Nico liked to be early as well as prompt. She picked up the mug of warm, simulated blood topped with whipped cream and drank.

"About the concert tonight," Nico then said, after she'd drunk half the contents of her cup. She found her napkin and dabbed bloody cream from her upper lip.

"Aye, that."

"You gave your Damara Airship tickets to who?" Nico asked.

"I gi'ed them tae the quine at the youth centre, chick," Shayla said. "The band's promotion company dinnae gie the lasses enough, so I added mine."

"But you're the lead singer's sister. It may be the biggest concert tour in the galaxy, but his people will give you more, right? I'm not insisting for Heloise and me." Nico's tone gentled. "I'm sure Shawn would really want you there."

"I want tae be there. But we three will at least see him backstage. Those passes, I still have."

Shayla's tone distanced, like it did whenever she spoke of seeing her younger brother. Nico was uncertain if that implied estrangement or Shayla harbouring fear of possible estrangement.

Nico wanted to say: Shawn doesn't blame you for Shy's death.

And if he did, he and Shayla needed to have that matter discussed.

If all else fails, she'll see him at his hotel before he flies out. Even if he is an intragalactic rock star. I'll make certain. I'll tell Heloise to make certain.

Nico glanced at her Id again. Shayla softly laughed.

"It may be an hour's flight from New London tae here, but you've time, love."

Nico rolled her eyes and put Dorothy away. "A shuttle can traverse this planet in only hours. But it still takes twenty-five minutes with one's legs to cover a mile and a quarter without a Makepeace's admonishment for running—"

"Fer runnin' like a vampire."

"Yes, for running like a vampire, when I've seen lizard people taking advantage with their speedy little ways *all the time*—but never mind. Heloise's arrival gate happens to be one of the farthest."

"Oh, ye're right, chick. Ye've so little time."

"Ha-ha." Nico smiled. "Heloise should be boarding soon. This business trip was only two days, but it felt like forever. Do you think the flowers are too much?" Nico fussed with the roses. "I ordered these through the hotel concierge. I didn't want simulated flowers."

"True roses and lilies, Niky?" Shayla touched her corsage, delighted. "That's pure quality, chick, she'll love them. I'm still wooin' her with my own bouquets."

"When you talk about seducing Heloise, it makes me so frisky." Shayla's gaze lit with mirth at Nico's silliness.

"Oh, I've already seduced her. A vampire auld as she needs remindin' often." The corner of Shayla's mouth crept up, a soft leer. She reached into her skirt's pocket and pulled out a loose roll of red satin ribbon, its width an inch.

"That's pretty," Nico admired the shade of red, the colour of fresh blood. "Are you wrapping something for her?"

"Only thing I'll be wrappin', chick…." Shayla unwound the ribbon. "Is 'eloise's wrists." She snapped the ribbon between her hands.

Nico's mouth formed an 'O'. She pulled out her Id and took a holo-snap of Shayla with the taut ribbon. Then she sent it to Heloise.

Shayla rewound the ribbon as Nico read Heloise's response.

"She's running like a vampire for her flight right now," Nico said.

Lucy's Diner stood one hundred feet from the nearest Jifk terminal and faced the airfield. But that day, the streamlined diner was filled with more than off-world travellers, tourists, and disorientated chrono-arrivals.

Nico persuaded Shayla to delay the start of her shift and remain behind the diner. She then entered through the bustling kitchen and stepped into the diner proper. Young Damara Airship fans in band tees and worn jeans crowded the tables and countertop seats.

Neo-hippies. Shouldn't they be waiting inside *Jifk for Damara Airship to arrive planet-side?* Peeved, Nico approached a group. If she strained her vampire's hearing in the diner's din, she might catch what they were discussing. Instead, she applied a skill she was practicing: lip reading. She focused on the scruffy boy the group paid rapt attention to.

Shawn O'Fey's sister, the boy's lips said.

Nico walked up to them.

After a few minutes, she rejoined Shayla at the outdoor break table.

"All those kids know you're Shawn's sister," Nico said sourly. "That's why they're in there. But I couldn't get rid of the bloody lot."

"Oh? Ya telt them Shawn's band was arrivin' now, didn't ya?" Shayla asked, her tone light.

"I did," Nico admitted. "And before you admonish me, it was in the best interest of freeing the tables of your stalkers. Those kids were barely buying coffee. Can you believe they offered me a toke to make me go away?"

Shayla laughed. Nico took the warm hand Shayla held out and reluctantly smiled. "They didn't believe me because they knew I was a vampire." Unlike Heloise, who could act warm and engaging, Nico had never shaken the effect of her deathly pallor—and the sinister reputation vampires automatically possessed. "When is Shawn due to arrive from out there?" She lifted her chin for above.

Shayla gently pulled her near. "Shawn and the rest are already planet-side, love," she whispered in Nico's ear, "at the Isle visiting friends and family. But aye, they're arriving in Again NewYork taeday. Only not at the intragalactic terminal."

Nico gasped. "They're coming to the domestic terminal? That's clever."

"Wheesht. Tell no one." Shayla winked. She rose and placed the wrapped flowers in Nico's arms.

"I've work tae return to, love," she said, apologetic. "And ye have 'eloise tae meet. Have I blessed ye, taeday, Niky?"

Nico shook her head, her smile giddy.

Shayla grinned and fished in her pocket. She brought out a Damara Airship pin-back bearing the band's symbol: the triangle holding the Y that denoted the dragon's eye. With solemnity, she pinned the black and purple one-inch button to the front of Nico's cardigan.

"Bless Nico Alexikova and Bear, beloved of Shayla O'Fey," Shayla intoned, "beloved of 'eloise Allen, and favoured of Darqueworld."

They kissed, Nico careful not to crush the flowers between them. She held Shayla's face when they parted.

"Treasure of Nico and Bear," she whispered to Shayla.

"Dorothy, play 'For Your Love,'" Nico requested, and put in her ear buds.

She entered Jifk spaceport and walked past Aleph Terminal's intragalactic check-in counters and the many off-world visitors who lumbered, slithered, darted, or rolled. An unobtrusive scan-net washed over her. If she allowed it, the scan could capture her personal data via the biometric tag embedded in the back of her left hand. A frisk by scan-net seemed tolerable in lieu of molestation at a physical security checkpoint. Without access to her bio-tag, the security scan could still discern her undead presence and the fact that she carried a switchblade tucked in the back of her skirt's waistband.

If she was not then in a hurry to traverse Aleph terminal for Beth, the terminal handling intragalactic connections via ferries to Nuit Four—Darqueworld's orbiting space station—Nico would have taken the time to mark the Other-beings around her, openly carrying their own weapons.

Magic wielders like Shayla and psionics like Esche were living weapons themselves, voluntarily holstering their abilities. The same was assumed of Other-beings like were-people and vampires. By that same reasoning, Darqueworld recognised beings that identified as warriors and let them travel with weapons. Nico was uncertain how ordinary civilians and off-worlders felt about that, but a bit of searching through Dorothy brought up no violent incidents at Jifk spaceport in the last six months. Either the unspoken and universal code of societal peace prevailed or the presence of security bots and the occasional Makepeace ensured no one acted like a jerk.

Nico made Bear wave to one broad-shouldered and lean, armoured Makepeace, the biomechanical being's helm gleaming. Though his mouth—one of those kissable ones Makepeace always seemed to have—remained impassive, his helm slowly turned, marking Nico's passage.

She summoned her *Spy The Makepeace* holo bingo cards in Dorothy and entered the Makepeace's collar number. Within the matched square, she chose body type, sex (he appeared to be mostly male) filled in unique characteristics, and nick-named him "Nick."

The game verified and approved her matched square. Nick had many entries of "hottie" by fellow Makepeace bingo players.

We all know they're bioengineered to have no genitals. But its fun to fantasise about their codpieces. She had enough lines filled to win a Makepeace pin-up calendar, several action figures, and their synth-pop album. But Nico had her own reasons for keeping records of the Makepeace, besides hoping she could win "super galactic house"—a sizeable jackpot—by filling in all 1,680 squares.

When she noticed young people—a mix of humans and off-worlders—in colourful knit hats and Damara Airship band shirts looking up at the arrivals holo-board of Beth terminal, she had a sudden thought.

"*Teh*," she emitted to Bear. "They should be stalking the first-class lounges. The band will probably arrive in something like a Concorde."

"Did you—did you just say, *Concorde?*" a dishevelled human man exclaimed, the lenses of his glasses cracked. He carried one of Immigration's *Welcome to Again New York* bags. He radiated body heat and perspiration. "Oh, what a relief to see someone from the later 20th century!" He held out a hand.

"Don't touch me," Nico automatically said, turning to keep her flowers away. "Uh—sorry. You shouldn't approach people who look like young girls," she further chastised. "Or who might be vampires. Welcome to Darqueworld." She hurried away for Gimel, the domestic flights terminal.

CHAPTER TWO

Unlike Aleph and Beth's terminals, where members of the intragalactic races milled along with chrono-arrivals dispersing from Immigration, Gimel was sedate (and architecturally—in Nico's opinion—dull). Ordinary humans were the majority present, many of whom being Darqueworld natives or settlers who barely, if at all, had need to travel the stars. The domestic terminal remained quiet while Aleph and Beth teemed. Perhaps the benign energy in Gimel was due to the near homogeny of the human-looking present, headed for familiar places rather than galactic parts unknown. Nico hadn't travelled beyond Again New York yet, but she hoped her first visit into space, once she'd saved enough for the trip, would be to Nuit Four.

"Hm." She looked at the first-class lounges she passed. "Dorothy, Jifk's Gimel terminal. Give me an executive lounge with exclusive access, celebrity clientele…members with an income range of—" She entered Heloise's net value. Then she thought of her lover's present style.

"Something cosmopolitan," she added.

Dorothy returned one result: Wayra's The Wing.

As she entered the corridor with the holo sign, *This way to G-Gates 01 to 20*, Nico requested the lounge's location. It lay across from the gate Wayra ships primarily used: Gate 10.

Nico looked up Wayra ships, an elite fleet of small but very swift planes possessing only first class seats and service. At Gate 10, she gave the black and polished surface of Wayra's executive lounge, simply branded "The Wing," a scrutinising eye. No scruffy youths in band shirts loitered outside.

"Hello, Damara Airship—if you're in there right now. Which I doubt, or else Shayla would've said. Obviously Heloise isn't a member yet since she's not arriving by Wayra," she told Bear.

Curiosity sated, she hummed and trotted for the faraway gate receiving Heloise's flight: Gate 84.

Twenty-five minutes later, Nico entered the section for Gates 71 through 88. She'd checked holo-boards along the way twice to make certain the words, *On Time*, glowed green by Heloise's flight number. Her Id pinged: the chime signalling a certain lover.

Heloise!

Nico pulled out Dorothy and read:

Hello, Doll. Saw a leviathan in the ocean. It had three heads.

Nico: *Did you put it in your Leviathan Bingo?*

Heloise: *Baby, the day I play bingo is when I use blue rinse.*

Nico: *I'm not using blue rinse.*

Heloise: *What music are you listening to?*

Nico sent Heloise the song, "Ten Miles High."

Heloise: *Oh, my adorable British Mod. Tell me you're wearing neo-*

Italian.

Nico: *I'm wearing a skinny tie. The Avians weren't British.*

Heloise: *Are you ready for Damara Airship?*

Nico shared about Shayla and their donated concert tickets.

After a discussion speculating about Shayla's motives, Heloise promised that she would get them into the concert. Reassured, Nico skipped to Gate 84.

Unlike the previous corridors she'd passed through, where spacious waiting areas filled both sides and attractive food and shopping modules lay between gate sections, gates 71 through 88 resembled a tacked on afterthought. Drab waiting areas lined the windows' side and boxy, small shops and food stands the other. Judging by the many empty seats in Gate 84's waiting area, Nico determined a flight had just left. A slouched space cowboy snored beneath his tipped down hat, a leather holstered pulse blaster strapped to his thigh.

Nico proceeded down the corridor and bypassed the holobook shop for the newsstand. There, kiosk-printed glossies and newspapers sat on display, convenient and familiar for chrono-immigrants used to paper products. She picked out a copy of *New Times* magazine with its Damara Airship cover.

After admiring the lead guitarist's flowing dress of embroidered flowers, Nico studied pretty Shawn O'Fey and the long-legged lads of the band, with their lengthy, curly hair, loosened shirts baring chests, and low slung, tight trousers, outlining more than a certain O'Fey sister would want pointed out to her.

"Oh, the gifts of psychedelic rock," Heloise had murmured when seeing the cover. "And I'm not talking about the music."

Nico could not say that she highly favoured intragalactic

rock herself, but she hadn't the chance on Old Earth to enjoy a super band's spectacle, weaving magic, mystery, and charisma on a captivated public.

"They should arrive soon," she mused to Bear. "Too bad we didn't figure this out sooner so Shayla could meet Shawn in The Wing lounge." A ventriloquist's dummy in a pink dress shirt and polka dot bow tie popped up behind the newsstand's counter.

Nico nearly swallowed her tongue.

His wooden hair painted a shiny red, the dummy's scratched, grey irises regarded the gate area proper. The corners of his red lips curled in a permanent smirk.

Don't look at him, don't look at him, don't look at him. Maybe he'll go away.

"Here you go." A customer carrying a *New Times* magazine presented a credit chit before the counter's mounted Id and scanned it. He touched his fedora to the dummy. "See you next week."

The customer departed, the dummy remaining still and silent as if it were a decorative sculpture.

Nico knew better. She stared at magazines and tried to feign the nonchalance Darqueworld residents seemed to possess regarding freaky, living and *mobile* wooden dummies.

That same attitude had been shown Mr Bear on their first arrival to Darqueworld. Bear was not an automaton, as the Victorian woman, Miss Fairditch, had thought, nor was he Nico's spirit guide, avatar, or totem animal, as Immigration had presumed. The only way she could explain Bear to Immigration was that Bear was her.

At least Shayla and Heloise understood. For the rest of Darqueworld's residents, they assumed that if Bear didn't walk or talk he was at least somehow aware.

Cognisant, like a certain *staring* ventriloquist's dummy.

The dummy's painted eyes had slowly slid to the side to regard Nico. Her shoulders stiffened.

I've just beaten heliophobia and catoptrophobia. I can do this.

She flipped through a vampire fetish magazine upside-down, then turned it right side up. Her Darqueworld Oth-er-beings etiquette handbook had said the proper term for animated creatures like the dummy was not "dummy" but *animistic inanimate obj—*

The dummy's hinged mouth dropped open.

"Howdy, miss!" he hollered.

Nico threw the magazine up in the air and ran away.

After Nico composed herself in the ladies room, she re-turned to a Gate 84 rapidly filling with travellers and visitors. A Makepeace had appeared, standing like a statue against the waiting area's wall. Long and sinewy, with the hint of high cheekbones beneath her helm, Nico thought she looked like Grace Jones. She nicknamed the Makepeace "Grace" in her bingo game, and then fetched black cat's eye frames from her shirt's breast pocket.

Donning them, Nico claimed a spot on the edge of the waiting area and stood as innocuously as possible with her flowers.

For her hotel front desk job, Heloise had gifted her with an invaluable tool: Id glasses. An Other-beings and off-world races encyclopaedia and identifier was downloaded to the glass, which would discreetly inform what was what of the various guests arriving for hotel check-in. Strange and un-familiar natural beings did not give her pause as much as humanoids her Id glass identified as simply human. Genetically altered and augmented, such humans, due to their personal customisations, often made Nico mistaken them for members of off-world humanoid species until her Id glass informed otherwise.

Nico focused her frames in the direction of a tall and scarred human male with cybernetic implants where his eyes once were. Much of his muscular torso and limbs were encased in a slender and malleable exoskeleton. The bootleg (and law enforcement exclusive) military and mercenary identifier in Nico's Id glass failed to classify his sort of cyborg. As the scarred man initiated a friendly and one-sided conversation with the impassive Makepeace, Nico's vampire hearing picked up his German.

Aw, scarred man's trying to bond with another biomechanical being.

Scarred man then turned, revealing the purpose of his exoskeleton. The components to a light cannon were embedded in the exo-frame of his broad back and limbs.

I wonder how fast his body can assemble that.

An older woman crossed Nico's vision, her long and wild hair pale and her face, paler. Her ice-blue eyes sat in dark sockets. She wore leather bracelets and necklaces with her flowing dress of earthy green.

Other-being identified, Nico's Id glass scrolled. *Banshee. Death's herald; wailer. Of possible faerie descent. Attributes: power shrieker. Possesses ability to fly. Named one of the top terror inducers—*

The woman glared, her gaze like a frigid wind.

Nico doffed her frames and put them in her shirt's breast pocket.

✈

When Nico checked the arrivals holo-board again, another ten minutes had been added to Heloise's arrival time.

Flights at other gates had taxied in, dropped off passengers, boarded more, and then departed. Nico resumed her spot near Gate 84, the windows outside showing no parked ship, and suppressed a yawn. Scarred man was still beside his new friend, the Grace Makepeace, when two human children ran up to her. Their brightly coloured Ids displayed holo bingo cards.

"We're playing Other-Being bingo," the boy declared. "Can we put you on our cards?"

The Makepeace acquiesced, and the mother, big bodied and with a bright scarf tied around her afro, guided her children with their holo interfaces.

"Write her collar number in that square," she bade the little girl. When their bingo squares flashed green, she prompted the children to thank the Makepeace.

"Thank you," they said in unison.

"You're welcome, young citizens," the Makepeace said, her voice deep and rich.

Oh my gods, she sounds like Grace Jones.

Nico summoned her own bingo game to add that note.

"There's a vampire," the little girl then said, pointing at Nico.

"No, I want that vampire," the boy said, already running to a leggy and deathly pale woman with a slit dress and flowing cape, departing from the next gate. Then he ran back to his mom. "Mama, she's a vampire, right?"

"I don't know, Taquan, you have to ask her. Keisha, c'mon," her mother called.

Nico made Bear wave at the little girl as she followed her family.

She glanced back at the arrivals board.

The holo-board's entry for Heloise's flight number glitched then perfected itself.

DELAYED, it read.

What? Nico blinked. The word remained, bright and red. Dorothy pinged.

Heloise wrote:

Hello Doll. I'm not there yet, I'm sorry.

They detoured and are putting us down in Sister Orleans.

Something about another plane needing our arrival gate.

I'll let you know when we're headed back again.

CHAPTER THREE

Delayed.

Nico sat on her barstool in the Punch Hut, flowers carefully laid aside on the bar top, and sighed. It had been half an hour since the gate announced the delay of Heloise's flight. Were her roses already drooping, looking as low as she felt?

She pulled out Dorothy and mournfully moved the entry, *trap Heloise in a janitor's closet and give her sex*, to "tentative" in her schedule. Then she looked at the last holo-snap Heloise had sent, of a cellophane-wrapped, red and white swirled lolly, held in Heloise's hand. Out of everything Heloise could have gotten Nico from New London the gift was perfect.

"Another?" the bartender asked, referring to the blood snack pack she'd sucked dry.

"No thank you," Nico said.

The Hut was a poor excuse for a bar, being a mere Tiki-style stand with its stools sitting in the corridor. It served booze, but in miniature sealed bottles, and Nico, who did not drink, only frequented Punch Huts because they sold the cheapest simulated blood snack packs in Jifk's terminals. A hairy, large wolf man drank bottle after tiny bottle of whisky beside her, sharing his troubles with the bartender. Nico had no idea why wolf man had a cricket bat strapped to his back and didn't care to ask.

He glanced over at her for the fourth time.

"Those roses are a beaut, mate—" he began.

"Don't touch my stuff."

The wolf man turned back and resumed his monologue with the bartender.

In the wall mirror behind the bartender, three leather-clad women walked by, catching Nico's eye.

One was a buxom redhead wearing bulky gloves and polished medals on her light-armoured chest. A boyish and sandy-haired woman in blue trailed behind her, two pulse pistols strapped to her thighs. Beside the gun woman, a black haired knife-thrower walked, a cross-body bandolier of black leather tight to her sternum, the six downward sheaths bearing the rounded handles of throwing knives.

Nico eyed the bandolier and discreetly adjusted Bear's harness.

The women's expressions appeared bored, as if they strolled simply for something to do. As the trio passed, Nico's gaze surreptitiously followed. A sheathed, nine inch blade sat rigged to the knife-thrower's lower back for a swift draw from below.

When the three turned around at the end of the section and returned, Nico swivelled on her stool to regard them openly. Circuit designs embedded the skin of the knife-thrower's hand.

Epidermal circuitry? Gleaming circuit traces followed the bones of the woman's slender fingers. *For enhanced speed and muscular control?*

If the sandy-haired woman bore the same skin circuitry, she covered them with black gloves. The trio neared.

"Hi," Nico said, addressing the knife-thrower. "I really like your bandolier."

The knife-thrower and her friends ignored her and walked by.

Nico fidgeted, feeling awkward.

"I wasn't going to kill you for it," she called after them.

When Nico swivelled back, the wolf man snorted.

"Good luck trying," he said. "Did you see that sheila's arc-light?"

"Arc-light?" Nico repeated. Dorothy pinged.

Heloise! She fetched her Id and read:

Doll, the blood coffee here is delicious.

Guess what? I was playing the bar's piano when the local vampire queen said 'hello.'

Heloise attached a holo-snap of an oval-faced African beauty, her peridot-green eyes glimmering.

"Wow." Nico showed the holo to Bear.

Nico: *Were you playing the blues?*

Heloise: *No, a Broadway tune. The queen showed me her big ruby, and Shayla's charm cracked!*

"Hey," Nico murmured. *Did she just try to mesmerise you?*

Heloise: *Yeah. No hard feelings, but she doesn't like 'no.'*

Nico snorted. Heloise could be pretty persistent herself.

"She probably sent us this photo in case she got kid-napped," she told Bear.

Heloise: *We're re-boarding! I'll see you soon.*

"Finally." *Don't get kidnapped. I love you.*

Heloise: *I love you too.*

Nico skipped away from the hut and headed for the near-est holo-board. As she searched for Heloise's flight update, a ship rolled slowly towards Gate 84, its engines powering down. The waiting area's occupants stirred.

"Her new arrival gate is Gate 7?" Nico exclaimed.

"Someone said Damara Airship is on this plane," a man remarked to his companion, and indicated the new arrival with his chin. "They switched to Gimel to avoid the paparazzi."

"Well, that's going to disappoint the kids lying in wait at the intragalactic terminals," his companion commented, wry.

Damara Airship, at this *gate?* An absurd choice, considering how far away they presently were from Gimel's own terminal exit. Nico glanced back at the holo-board. The flight disembarking right then had flown in from the Isle.

She entered the waiting area to get a better view of the arriving passengers. Ahead of her sat the space cowboy and the mother with her two playing children. The cowboy rose and stretched, and the scarred man turned from the Makepeace to regard the boarding doors. Nico moved past the cowboy as Taquan made engine sounds, arcing a toy ship through the air, and Keisha skipped backwards. With a gentle hand, Nico prevented the little girl from colliding with her.

The boarding doors slowly swung open.

Distant, high-pitched laughter issued.

Winged sprites erupted from the opening, tiny as locust and swarming. They shrieked as twisted little creatures hopped madly after. In the billowing dust cloud that followed and expanded in the gate area, bright colours and sparkling motes swirled.

"*DIE FEE,*" the scarred man shouted.

The faerie?!

Nico drew her switchblade.

The screeching laughter inundated. Grinning winged creatures fast approached and then blipped out before her, swallowed up by reality's veil suddenly dropping down. The coming cloud bloomed.

It hit, flooding Nico's sight with giant and warm light-bubbles of pulsing colours. Her vision warped as the bubbles popped. A drawn gun brushed against leather behind her.

Nico spun as the cowboy aimed at the children.

She flung her blade.

It struck the gun, and she tackled the kids to the floor. A wild pulse blast ricocheted off the gate seats and singed her hair. Melted plastic pelted.

"What are you doing, shooting at kids?" Nico yelled.

"Kids?" the cowboy said, aghast. More coloured bubbles popped, hazing him. "They're hobgoblins!"

The haze faded and a tall and grizzled knocker in miner's garb—with the same aghast expression as the cowboy—stood in his place.

Nico gaped. She looked down. Grey faces with pointy ears and big, frightened eyes stared up at her.

"Keisha, Taquan?" their mother called, frantic. She crawled across the floor towards them, a big-breasted hobgoblin in a colourful headscarf.

"Mama, an *elf* is on top of us," one of the hobgoblins yelled in Taquan's voice.

"No, it's the vampire," the other child said. Keisha touched Bear.

Nico and the hobgoblin mother stared at each other.

"Get off my—" the mother threatened, bringing her handbag up.

"Citizens," the Makepeace boomed, her deep voice magnified. "There has been a glamour-attack. Drop your weapons before you harm each other. There has been a glamour-attack. Drop your—"

Nico quickly rose.

Where Grace Makepeace once stood, a shining elf queen levitated, hair flowing and her visage terrifying. She raised her hand and people scurried, screaming. The bulky troll next to her scrambled back. Weapon components rose from his body and assembled into a cannon.

That's not a troll—it's scarred man—

He fired.

The blast thundered, shaking windows. The streak of white that was the elf queen's body ploughed into the gate's counter and wall and caved them in. Debris dust rose, and with it, disintegrating flashes of sparkling motes. The Makepeace lay in the wreckage, still and silent.

"*Ach nein,*" scarred man shouted in horror. "*Ich schoss ein Makepeace!*"

"Ya idiot, of course ya shot a Makepeace. We've been *beguiled,*" a woman cried. Nico swivelled, seeing only a column and palms. The woman's mature and thick brogue did not belong to Shayla. "The Makepeace said tae drop yer—don't be pointin' yer cannon at *me!*"

An unearthly scream launched from the woman's direction. It drove through the gate area, a shrill blast that detonated against the scarred man, sending him flying. His massive gun disassembled. Nico bit down on her flowers' wrapping and snatched up the children. She leapt over the seats and away from the altercation, the mother scrambling after her.

"Ssstop sscreeching, bansheee," a woman berated.

"Don't be tellin' me what tae do, ya spittin'—" the banshee hollered.

Bloody hell. Nico barrelled across the corridor for a souvenir shop. Spewing acid hissed and another harrowing scream erupted, the aural volley slamming into the gift shop's win-

dow. It vibrated, wobbling the reflection of a wide-eyed and
black haired elf carrying flowers in her mouth and hobgoblin children under her arms.

The glass shattered. Nico skidded into the shop and ducked
behind the counter. The banshee's hair-whitening sound
drove dread deep into her bones. The flowers dropped from
her mouth.

Argh—it's like Esche's mind-scream.

"It's okay," Nico said shakily as the cowering kids burst
into tears. She shook and fought the terror. "If Bear wasn't a
vampire, he'd wet his shorts too." She made Bear dance for
them.

Their mother scurried behind the counter and hugged the
children.

"Ya spittin' cobra! This was my best dress!" the banshee
shouted.

"Ladies, have you need of assistance?" a digitised voice
interrupted.

"Shut up, robot," the banshee threatened.

While the gate attendant calmly responded, Nico trembled
and examined her flowers. Her fangs had broken out and
punctured the paper.

Someone stumbled into the shop. A hulking ogre tottered,
his immense features and round-eyed gaze looking as fright-
shocked as Nico felt. He smelled of liquor.

Nico stood and grabbed a bobble head of Again NewY-
ork's mayor.

"An elf," the ogre said and pulled a cricket bat from his
back.

A cricket bat?

"Wait, I'm not an elf," Nico yelled. "And you're not an
ogre!"

"A what?" the ogre said. Nico dropped the bobble head and jumped the counter. She ducked beneath his brandished bat and swung up.

Her fist connected with his chin, the sound cracking. As the ogre's head snapped back, his guise disintegrated, becoming flying dust motes and light specks. The wolf man crumpled to the floor.

How long did a glamour-attack's effect last? She looked furtively towards the shattered window. A malevolent, little bearded face laughed among the cluster of souvenir Damara Airship teddy bears before the window.

If that isn't a real *faerie*—

Nico grabbed an *I Love Again NewYork* snow globe and hurled it.

The globe walloped the fellow on the forehead. He howled amid falling teddy bears and then blipped from view. Nico ran up and found no trace of his presence.

Was it possible to kill a faerie? The hazed air lightened, the buoyant lights and colours of the glamour attack fading from the corridor and gate area outside. The guises cloaking those present disintegrated into winking dust, leaving dazed victims. Fabric suddenly brushed the back of Nico's head, and she flinched, startled.

A naked, winged female, no bigger than a handheld statuette, lugged a Damara Airship tee shirt, stripped from a teddy bear. She flew out the shattered window and winked out, returned to the invisible realm.

Nico looked down. All the teddy bears no longer wore tee shirts.

When she retrieved her flowers from behind the counter, the huddled family was human once more. Nico touched her Id, stored behind Bear.

"Dorothy, locate my blade," she shakily requested and cautiously reentered the gate proper.

CHAPTER FOUR

"Welcome to Gimel Terminal," the calm male voice of Gimel's BRAI—Basic2 Responsive Artificial Intelligence—said over the intercom. "An incident has occurred affecting all Gimel gates. I repeat, all Gimel gates are affected. Flights will cease loading and unloading of passengers until the matter is dealt with. We ask that you remain where you are until the matter is dealt with. Thank you for your patience while we resolve the matter quickly."

A barrier door rolled down before Gate 84's boarding doors, sealing it. Nico looked down the corridor and saw more gate barriers descending. Exiting passengers hurried to crawl out from beneath them before they shut. The scrambling reminded Nico of old Berlin Wall footage, when people escaped for the city's west side.

"They're sealing us in!" someone shouted.

"No, they're not. They're keeping the arrivals *out*," another clarified.

"I'm getting out of here," the first person said.

"Not after punching me during the glamour attack, you're not," a third person threatened.

Nico rolled her eyes as a scuffle broke out. She fetched her switchblade from beneath chair wreckage.

"I'm…" The cowboy approached her, contrite. "I'm really sorry—"

"Tell that to the kids," Nico said tersely as she shut her blade. She pointed towards the shop. "They're in there. You should buy them ice cream."

The cowboy nodded.

"Flights will cease disembarking until the incident affecting all gates is resolved," the BRAI announced. "Thank you for your patience. Enjoy our many shops and satisfying intragalactic cuisines while you wait. We ask that you remain where you are until the incident is dealt with."

Scarred man sat hunched in the gate counter's debris, keeping vigil over the inert body of Grace Makepeace. Nico frowned.

Why is she still inactive? Scarred man's cannon would have taken out Nico with no problem, but an armoured Makepeace was designed to defeat warrior class Other-beings. Nico had watched enough Makepeace battle footage to know that they did not go down easily.

"Thank you for travelling with us," the BRAI continued. "Thank you. Thank you. Thank you. Mind the gap."

People raised their heads.

"Mind-mind-mind-mind—"

The voice cut off.

Hushed whispers echoed what Nico was thinking: what could cause a BRAI to malfunction?

"I-I'm getting out of here," someone repeated with uncertainty.

Voices rose. Human gate attendants shouted as well, repeating the BRAI's message. Nico stepped aside with her flowers held near and her back to a column, assessing those who might panic. Without a Makepeace's calm presence to maintain authority, she didn't feel like hanging around.

Her vampire's hearing perked.

"It's not just the BRAI, the emergency exits aren't functioning."

The tense whisper belonged to a sharply dressed stewardess, her head close to her fellow flight attendant's, both having waited at Gate 84 for their own flights.

"The last instruction was to remain where we are. But I don't think Gimel wants us trapped in here with the fae," her companion whispered back. "It creates a hostage situation."

"I agree. Our first priority is everyone's safety."

Red lights flashed outside, and people rushed to the windows to look at the emergency vehicles arriving.

"Let's see if a gate computer's working," the stewardess then suggested.

Nico debated throwing her fate in with the stewardesses, who might find a way to evacuate to the tarmac. She immediately dismissed the option.

Her priority was to meet Heloise—especially with hooligan faeries running amok. She shook herself out. Dread still lingered in her bones from the banshee's scream. A quick survey of the corridor marked the woman sitting at the Punch Hut, glowering. Dorothy pinged.

Nico pulled her Id out from behind Bear.

Shayla: *Love, Lucy's heard of trouble. What's happening in Gimel?*

Nico: *Fae came on the plane.* She explained the situation as quickly as her fingers could type.

I'm coming now, Shayla typed back.

Nico blew breath and silently berated herself. She hated bringing trouble to Shayla when her lover had her brother's visit to feel anxious about, but Nico was out of her depth with glamour-bombing faeries.

And Shayla, as a witch of the Isle and a coven's ex-gun-slinger, would not ignore a situation like the one Nico was presently in.

Thank you, Nico typed in gratitude. *But why did they come on the plane? What do they want?*

Shayla: *Who can ken? Perhaps someone got away and they've come for that one.*

Nico shivered. It hadn't occurred to her that the tales of fae kidnapping children might be real.

Nico: *Heloise is arriving at a different gate. I'm going there now.*

Shayla: *Protect yourself. Stay away from the faerie kind. Those folk mean mischief and madness is their gift.*

Nico nodded and sent back an affirmation: *I'll be careful.*

The earlier gates did not fare better than Gate 84. Nico concentrated on watching the gate numbers diminish even as she noted the damage that had been swiftly wrought by beguiling faeries.

Gate 80—

Gate 76—

Each passing gate suffered walls burnt by pulse blasts, seats wrecked by fighting, and smouldering carpeting. People hobbled in the smoke or lay wounded. Nico looked around for security bots that could help. A grey and black unit stood inert, its lights and holo-bulletin turned off. Another rolled in a tight circle as people scurried around it, alarmed.

MIND THE GAP, its holo-bulletin flashed, then the image sputtered and died.

The unit rolled to a dead stop.

Why are they malfunctioning? Nico inhaled for any trace of the ozone-like scent of an electrical or lightning attack from an elemental Other-being, but knew the units were well-shielded. If the bots were deactivating, the telepresence of Gimel's BRAI—and any remote personnel—would cease.

And the cameras? Nico looked up at one nestled high above a waiting area. With the BRAI down, its cameras might also be down. Would anyone still know how bad it was inside Gimel?

The stewardesses were right to try and find a way out.

She returned her attention to the corridor's chaos. A dazed and kneeling man slowly gathered the green stems of his scattered bouquet, the blooms bitten off.

Nico quickly counted her roses and lilies. When she stepped into the section where eateries lay—and the remnants of a food battle—the banshee sat at another Punch Hut.

Nico glanced at the section she'd left, then at the banshee again.

"Can you turn invisible?" she demanded, addressing the woman. "Go into the faerie realm, like—like the ones that arrived at Gate 84?"

"What?" The banshee glared. "Don't be insultin'. I flew here, ya jakey bam. They were all out of whiskey at the other hut." She lifted a miniature bottle to her lips.

Yeah, and you're probably fleeing the scene of your fight. "Well, you are related to the fae, right? I just thought you could—" Nico's eyes widened. "Wait a minute. You can *see* them, can't you?" She looked around. People stood about, relatively unmolested. No invisible mischief seemed afoot. "Why did they come on the plane? What do they want?" She stepped towards the banshee.

"Back off, revenant," the woman snapped. "No good

comes of bein' curious about them. Leave it be."

"I've a friend—a *lover*—who will deal with them when they try to exit Gimel, and every bit of information helps," Nico pressed.

"*I'll* tell you," the banshee bit out. She poked Nico on her Damara Airship button. "Ye're all a bunch of bampots, that's what. Running after longhaired boys with their instruments. Gettin' blootered on *shrooms*. Them and *you*. It's *stupid*."

Nico gazed in amazement as the banshee returned her attention to her tiny bottle.

"Okay, thanks," Nico said.

For nothing. She left the woman to her drinking and followed the holo sign: *This way to G-Gates 70 to 61*.

Madness possessed the next section.

The spacious gates on either side, with their sunken waiting areas and palms, still retained the colour-fog of a glamour bomb, the cloud thickly gathered at the section's end. Terrified people yelled, accusing. Nico's nose twitched.

She smelled death somewhere, faint and faraway. It was the trace of life's hot liquid, soaking the ground.

"Look at me—look at me," a giant toad wailed, webbed hands to his head. He dripped pond water and was bedraggled with wet rushes.

Nico ignored him, his guise slowly disintegrating. She figured the man would be upset long after his time as a toad.

As she advanced, the glamours continued to fragment. She glimpsed her own reflection in the polished surface of one of the columns. The face that glanced back had unruly and short black hair with high pointed ears. She stopped to stare into her own eyes.

They had remained grey—larger than her own eyes—and in their depths, seemed to reflect more; things she did not personally know. Timeless outcrops and subterranean kingdoms. Windswept skies and rock strewn lands. She took a holo-snap of her faerie self before her guise disintegrated. Then she noticed the legs of a Makepeace, stuck out of a concrete wall at Gate 68.

A huge and tattooed man stood next to the legs, his bearded head hanging. The last sparkling particles of a glamour fell from his body. A bear's skin rested on his shoulders and a great and cracked war club lay at his feet.

"I'm so sorry," the bear man whispered hoarsely. He wiped at the big tears that streaked his cheeks. "I—I thought him the *erlking*."

The Elf King? Nico's hand nearly edged for her blade. Then she chastised herself. *The real elf king doesn't eat people...or does he?*

"It's all right, son. The Makepeace can self-repair," an old man consoled. "He's probably doing it right now."

"Faeries have everyone more than spooked," Nico muttered to Bear. "Even tough Other-beings."

She left the gate, the Makepeace still inert.

In the gates ahead, the glamour bomb's full effect and the scent of death remained. Coloured bubbles and twinkling motes densely drifted, a cloud she couldn't avoid even if she crawled on the floor. She realised who she might be catching up to.

Makepeace are always in contact with each other. Even without telepresence or cameras, they'll at least know two of their own went down. She was certain they would prepare accordingly. A Makepeace and fae confrontation was due to happen ahead, if not already.

She stilled her lungs and walked into the cloud.

At the far end of the corridor, frantic people ran into the section, faerie guises enveloping them. Nico focused her vampire's hearing to catch their voices.

"We can't evacuate," one panted.

"What do you mean?" someone called. "This isn't like a space station, with emergency section barriers brought down. Are we trapped?"

"No, not like that—something, something got to the others," one of the returnees said. "We're not going back there."

Nico quickened her pace.

A bedraggled and shaggy haired boggart stood at an abandoned noodle cart, slurping down the cooked prawns. He spun to look at her, his eyes the size of saucers. Nico jumped back.

"Did you pay for that?" she snapped, and brought her free fist up. She held her flowers away. For one moment, she wondered if true faerie were lurking among them. The boggart's guise was too convincing.

"Elf," the boggart uttered, his hot breath smelling of fish.

"I am not."

"Are you sure?" he said.

"I'm not an elf," Nico yelled. "Are you a bogie?"

"No, I'm a walrus," the boggart protested.

"A were-walrus?" Nico exclaimed. "No bogie could make that up."

Dorothy pinged. Nico dropped her fist.

"Excuse me," she said to the boggart, and pulled out her Id. She walked away.

Shayla's message read:

Security closed access to Gimel's gates and won't let me enter. Do you see any of the Aos Sí?

The bigger fae? Nico typed. *They may be ahead of me.*

Shayla: *Avoid them. Dinna let them see you.*

Nico: *Ok. How is security going to handle this? Or the Makepeace?*

A thought then occurred to her: the emergency vehicles in Gate 84's section. If she were security or the Makepeace, she'd gain access from there and close in from behind, trapping the fae.

Nico looked in the direction she'd left, seeing nothing but despondent and hurt travellers within the glamour cloud.

"Or maybe not," she murmured to Bear, and resumed reading.

Shayla: *I dinna ken. Gimel's security overrules the Makepeace here, Love, and I'm only a waitress to the security head.*

"Idiots," Nico muttered. She indulged in the regret she shared with Heloise of Shayla's continued reluctance to resume her old role as a coven's pistol and peacekeeper. The help of a weird matter wielder of Shayla's calibre was necessary for the matter in hand, in her estimation.

Shayla: *Either they stop the* Aos Sí *within Gimel or the* Aos Sí *exits. I'm betting the latter, and I'll be here to greet them.*

Nico: *Ok. Security hasn't a clue what they're dealing with, do they?*

Shayla: *The security head here doesn't believe, Love, even with the Makepeace explaining. His own eyes and the cameras dinna give him proof the wee ones exist.*

"I bet he's one of *those* humans," Nico said to Bear, "just can't ever believe in leprechauns and lucky charms." But she nearly couldn't fault the man. If she hadn't seen the fae disembark herself, she might have disbelieved.

She sent Shayla her elf photograph.

Shayla: *Niky.*

Nico's dead heart swelled.

Shayla: *The glamour captures you perfectly, Love. It's magic.*

"Magic" in Scots slang meant "great." Chuffed, Nico sent Shayla animated hearts.

Shayla: *Also, I've tickets again. Be ready for the concert tonight.*

"Yay," Nico said to Bear. She sent Shayla a shooting pistol animation.

Wheesht, Shayla typed back.

When Nico raised her gaze, her grin faded.

The source of the death scent suffused the last gate. A male hobgoblin in a dark suit and tie lay on his side, alone in a shunned waiting area, his dead eyes wide. His chest wound exsanguinated into the soaked carpeting.

Nico's fangs elongated at the sight of so much spilt blood— human blood. The aura of murder clung. Nico walked over to him, a human male wearing sensible, dark shoes; law enforcement shoes.

In death, he looked surprised. She reached down and shut his eyelids. His back also bled, the wound a clean and tidy exit.

A projectile weapon didn't do this.

She flicked his suit jacket open. On the belt of his trousers, a marshal's silver badge gleamed. His gun remained snapped in his shoulder holster.

She took a holo snapshot.

A soft-shod foot brushed carpeting behind her. Nico put her fangs away and turned.

A longhaired nixie stood, dripping water.

Luminous-eyed, the nixie swiftly drew a short, straight sword from the sheath strapped to her back.

Nico's free hand fell loose to her side.

She noted the sword's square guard.

A ninjato *wielded by a water spirit? Yeah, right.*

"We've been glamour-bombed," Nico barked. "Stand down."

"So you're not a—" the nixie said warily.

"No, I'm not." Nico bypassed the nixie and approached the exit. Nixie-woman didn't yet know Nico was a vampire. If she chose to attack, Nico doubted she'd try beheading first.

Especially before all the witnesses.

Soft footsteps padded behind her. Nico whirled.

The nixie stood with her sword back in its sheath. Standing at the edge of the gates' section, her guise slowly fragmented, revealing a human woman with black hair and wearing loose clothing. On her feet, she wore *jika-tabi*. She stared at Nico, her gaze inscrutable.

"We're going the same way," the swordswoman said. She shrugged.

"Fine," Nico said.

She stepped out of the section, her new companion's gaze boring holes into Nico's back. Nico followed the holo-sign, *This way to G-Gates 60 to 48.*

The moving walkways connecting to gates 60 through 48 were deserted and littered with abandoned baggage. Nico ignored her wary tagalong and pulled out her Id.

Hi, how are you? she typed to Heloise.

Heloise: *I'm sitting smack dab in the middle of First Land. They set us down again, darling. I see Gimel's having pixie dust trouble.*

Nico: *Oh?*

Heloise: *I'm monitoring certain communications.*

Nico: *You Mata Hari.* She was unsurprised that her lover

knew how to access and eavesdrop on spaceport security
com nets. She sent Heloise her elf holo-snap.

Heloise: *Grr, you look delicious. Stay away from real elves now.*

Nico: *Is there a tech-ware that can help me see real elves?*

Heloise affirmed and told her what to search for, and Nico
thanked her with a dancing bat animation.

"Are you going to get on the walkway or what?" the swordswoman suddenly demanded as Nico ended her conversation.
She'd nearly forgotten about the woman—almost.

"You could go ahead of me," Nico suggested. She drew
her cat's eye frames from her shirt's breast pocket, flicked
them open, and donned them.

"Safety in numbers," the swordswoman said, smiling. Nico
ignored her attempt at charm and stepped on to the moving
walkway. Her companion followed.

"Dorothy, recommend a perception filter for my Id glass,
one that can discern the faerie realm—the real realm, not
virtual."

"Second Sight Specs," Dorothy said as an animated holo-
ad played, "is your ultimate faerie de-cloaking ware. Over
300 five star ratings and voted Best New Ware on the Isle.
Want to know what's causing mischief or movement in the
home or in your life? Now, with instant perception detec-
tion for hidden brownies, sprites, pixies, phoukas, bogies,
and more, Second Sight Specs opens their world to you. De-
cloak higher Fae with specialised targeting—"

"Yes, this ware," Nico said. "Download, please."

Dorothy quoted a price.

Nico groaned. Paycheques went up in smoke in her mind's
eye. "Okay, fine."

"Downloading," Dorothy responded.

If we get to visit Shayla's home on the Isle, this ware will come in handy, Nico mentally grumbled to Bear. She stepped off the walkway, the swordswoman behind her. The corridor ahead turned right. Nico sucked in breath, tasting the hint of something sweet and chemically tinted. It was slightly touched by the aroma of wet paper towels.

Her vampire's hearing picked up nothing. She glanced at the swordswoman, who stood with a hand on her sword's handle.

"What?" the swordswoman said in a low voice. "I'm not blade-happy, if that's what you're thinking."

"I'm not thinking anything."

Nico remained where she was, unblinking, until the swordswoman straightened and let go of her sword.

"Happy?" the swordswoman said.

"There could be kids ahead, you know," Nico berated.

"Yeah? Well, if there's trouble, you should ditch those flowers."

Nico's gaze iced.

The woman held her hands up. "I'm sure the person those are for will love them."

Nico gave her a parting glare as she resumed their approach. "Id glass, remove any guises and glamours while scanning."

"Need a glamour unscrambler? Add on Glamour Annihilator for another—" Dorothy said from behind Bear.

"Dorothy, end ad."

I'll just use vampire instinct.

She turned down the corridor, the swordswoman moving cautiously in the rear. A damp, sweet smell engulfed.

"Wait, that's—" The swordswoman scrambled back.

Nico lunged and grabbed the woman. She hauled her up and flung her down the darkened passageway.

A thud sounded, then strangled gasps as hands and feet

desperately scrambled. Nico froze her lungs, shut her lips tight, and walked in.

The section's air was still and silent. Flickering lights lit gates made dark by emergency shields brought down over the windows. Far ahead, fallen bodies littered; the evacuees who didn't quite make it out.

Knockout gas.

A pile of Other-beings and humans blocked Nico as if they too had recently stepped into the section, only to fall victim to the gas.

So that's what happened to the escapees from the last section.

At the top of the pile, the swordswoman lay, insensate.

Nico laid her flowers aside and pulled out her black marker from behind Bear. She carefully spelled out MURDERER on the woman's face.

After taking the woman's photo and sending it and an account of the dead marshal to terminal security, Nico climbed over the pile of fallen people. The Makepeace who had released the suppression gas lay alone in the corridor, her helm's faceplate sealing her mouth and chin shut. Nico soberly studied her body for injury. She saw none.

Please don't be dead. Even when they stood about like statues, watching over Again NewYork, Nico felt that Makepeace were always aware. Somehow that focused presence was missing from the Makepeace lying before her.

A lone security bot slowly manoeuvred around abandoned possessions, its lights blinking. Its holo bulletin projected: EVACUATE.

It rolled for the inert Makepeace. Nico surveyed the area for un-living like herself…a vampire indulging in an illegal snack, perhaps. Even the android gate attendants were shut down.

No faerie kind detected, her Id glass gave.

The gas took out everyone but the invisible folk. Faeries, three, Make-peace, zero.

She returned her attention to the Makepeace. The bot's scanning beam moved along the Makepeace's helm.

Nico's Id glass activated.

Ant-sized dots squeezed out from beneath the Make-peace's chest armour and swelled into tiny and stout brown-clad men, rough looking and carrying tiny tools.

Id glass: *Faerie kind detected. Brownies. Domestic spirits skilled in repair, mechanics, and artisan crafts. Require libations to be appeased. Will take offence at references to payment or labour—*

Nico back-pedalled as the brownies leapt for the security bot and winked to ant-size again, swarming into the robot's crevices. The security bot shook.

Nico jumped over the Makepeace's body and bypassed the bot as it began to spin.

MIND THE GAP, MIND THE GAP its bulletin repeated.

She hurried to a safe distance and pulled out her Id.

The Makepeace are down and the security bots too, she typed to Shayla. *Brownies did it.*

Shayla answered immediately.

Shayla: *Very bad. Stay away or they'll dismember ya, for they'll ken you're un-living, understand?*

Nico: *Yes'm.*

Shayla: *I'll have fresh milk delivered to lure them. How did you see the little ones? Shy had second sight, not me. Shawn has it too. I need a spell to see them.*

Nico explained about her Second Sight ware, and Shayla thanked her.

Shayla: *And dinna let the bigger faerie see you. Avoid them. Are you still good, Love?*

I am. Nico sent her a purring kitten animation.

"Hey! Hey, wait up," a boyish voice yelled, disrupting the quiet.

Nico spun. The ventriloquist's dummy from the newsstand clambered over the swordswoman's body, then trotted towards Nico on odd, jerky legs. He stopped before the fallen Makepeace.

"Another Makepeace down?" he exclaimed, and his wooden hands waved. "Crazy! These faeries mean business!" The dummy pulled himself up, his painted eyes rolling aside to look at Nico. "If you're trying to exit Gimel, you shouldn't go alone. I'll come with you!"

Nico shook her head rapidly, her undead stomach in her throat. If the dummy came any nearer she might kick it.

"I may be wooden and I can't get hurt like you flesh-types, but boy, do these faeries have me rattled!" He rattled in emphasis, hinged jaw clapping. He then leapt over the Makepeace, the malfunctioning security bot still spinning. Nico scurried back.

"Besides, I work here," he said, "I know a faster way out. You take the—"

Brownies detected, Nico's Id glass flashed.

Brown dots swarmed out from beneath the security bot's plating and leapt for the dummy. The tiny bodies grew.

"AHHH," the dummy screamed as little brown men landed and clung to him. Minuscule blades flashed as the little men swiftly brought down axes.

"AHHH, stop!" They buried their blades in his face.

"Stop chopping meeee," he screamed and ran with flailing arms at Nico.

Nico fled.

The dummy pursued, shrieking. Nico raced for a column

and swerved around it. The dummy collided and collapsed. His waving arm abruptly dropped beneath the brownies' flashing blades and fell off, the threads of his severed cotton shirt fraying.

A wrapped gift basket with cheese and wine lay near. The dummy screeched, his face muffled by tiny men. Nico tore the basket's wrapping.

She wrested the cheese round out and ripped the vacuumed packaging with her fangs. She tossed the naked cheese near the fiercely chopping brownies.

A few swarmed for the cheese and chopped at it. The rest continued with their work, ignoring an offering with perhaps too many preservatives for their discerning palate. Beneath their axes, the dummy lay silenced, his grey eyes obliterated. The brownies rapidly rendered his red lips into flying chips.

Nico backed away.

She turned and ran. Over the tiny and rapid sounds of furious axes, the security bot tumbled over.

CHAPTER FIVE

Nico jumped onto the next stretch of deserted moving walkways and made herself halt. She was prepared to flee with a vampire's speed all the way to Gate 7 and leave behind the sounds of a wooden dummy being murdered, but running into the higher faeries was what Shayla had told her not to do. A pulse pistol screamed abruptly ahead.

Nico's head snapped up.

Nothing more sounded. A fading glamour-cloud drifted at the walkway's end.

Nico brought her switchblade up as she rolled towards it.

The cloud dissipated in a slow shower of glinting gold.

She stepped off.

Three women lay in the passageway before her, bodies askew: the armed trio Nico had seen at the Punch Hut. The knife-thrower sat slumped with burnt head bowed, her back against a wall smeared with her blood.

Oh no.

Nico opened her lungs and tasted the air. Gas was no longer present, but the fresh smell of spilt blood permeated. Her fangs broke out.

She tamped down her automatic snarl as she approached. The energy of violence had yet to dispel. Each woman lay at a distance from each other that formed a triangle between them: a Mexican standoff.

Nico paused by the knife-thrower. The woman had faced the sandy-haired one, who lay at the base of the opposite wall. The redhead had fallen farther down the corridor, body thrown back by a knife deep in her throat and a pulse-blast disfiguring her face. The knife-thrower and the gun woman had killed the redhead together, and then turned on each other.

Nico slowly knelt, put her blade away, and laid her flowers aside, hoping to sense a weak pulse or scant breath from the knife-thrower. Nico knew death; the soul had fled.

"I'm sorry," she said.

The dead woman reared up and stabbed Nico below the ribs.

Nico gripped the woman's wrist as her muscles seized around the nine-inch blade.

Bloody hel—pre-programmed attack reflex!

"My best *outfit*," Nico ejected. She socked the knife-thrower.

Whatever battery fuelled the dead woman's skin circuitry kept her knife hand moving forwards, attempting to bury the blade. Nico squeezed and crushed the wrist and its circuit traces.

Attack sequence interrupted, the woman's body slumped, her blade slicing more of Nico's dead colon before she could yank it out. Had she not trapped the woman's wrist, the attack's completion would have been the knife pulled across Nico's belly—amputating Bear—and disemboweling her.

"I wasn't going to *bite* you," she ground out. She grabbed

her flowers and stumbled away. Hand pressed against the entry wound, she focused on healing the opening before she bled more on her clothes.

Her foot trod on the sandy-haired woman's gun hand.

The hand jerked up, finger pulling the trigger. Nico leapt.

She back-flipped over a pulse blast that ricocheted off the corridor wall. Nico drew her blade in midair and threw. It pinned the dead woman's wrist to the floor. Shots hit the wall.

The second pre-programmed hand brought up its pistol.

Nico stomped the hand down, and the corridor lit from two pulse pistols rapidly firing. She shielded her flowers.

After what seemed an eternity, the pistols ran out of energy. Nico wearily lifted her foot and pulled her knife out of the dead woman's wrist. The woman's fingers continued to pull on the triggers as she brought the emptied guns up and aimed at Nico.

She slapped them away. "Booby-trapping your own bodies is *not cool*," she told the dead women. Then she bent over and retched.

Her sliced guts, still knitting, made obscene, squishy sounds. Nico had yet to outgrow her nauseous reaction to messy internal healing—especially from gunshot wounds.

"Ughh. At least it's not bone fragments coming back together," she told Bear.

Cautious footfall echoed in the walkway area.

Nico looked towards the gassed section. A male vampire couple had entered, arm in arm and dressed in black—one in a frock coat and the other in gleaming latex. Even at that distance, Nico could spy their aloof expressions. They looked about calmly, and then noticed Nico.

"Don't come through here. It's booby-trapped," she yelled.

The Goth couple turned and hurried back into the gassed section.

"Right, thanks for the help," Nico said. "Dorothy, tell me what an arc-light weapon is." She pulled out her black marker.

"The arc-light: high frequency electrical discharge weapon with two part ignition," Dorothy said. "Can deliver 100 centimeters of brush discharge, or approximately 3.6 megajoules of power."

Nico spelt out WARNING, BOOBY TRAPPED, on the floor leading into the trio's shot-up passageway.

She sighed. "3.6 megajoules, huh? What is the redhead, a human Tesla coil? Don't answer that."

She studied how the dead redhead blocked the passageway's end.

"Lightning moves faster than a vampire," she told Bear soberly. Her Id chimed.

Nico pulled Dorothy out and read:

Hello, Doll. Have the elves kidnapped you?

Nico: *Nope, I'm still a free vampire.*

Heloise: *Shayla's shared more about what's happening. Are you doing as she told you?*

Nico could imagine Heloise's grin.

Nico: *I don't want to be admonished. Why do you think the fae came on the plane?*

Heloise: *First guess? They want something back. They're tricky little things, a lot like you, so be careful.*

Nico: *Yes, Mommy.*

Heloise: *Tease. We're leaving First Land, finally. This must mean the Makepeace will resolve the issue before we get there.*

Nico: *Ok. Are you and Shayla exchanging vulgar messages?*

Heloise: *Of course. We don't want to singe your delicate ears, baby.*

"Pfft," Nico ejected, rolling her eyes. *I'll be at your gate waiting.* She sent Heloise her elf photo decorated with animated love-bats.

Ending the conversation, she walked over to the dead gun woman, the trigger fingers still twitching.

"Here goes," she announced to Bear, and hefted the gun woman up by the nape. She hurled her towards the passageway's end.

The redhead's gloved hands shot up, a crackling arc of dazzling light forming between her palms. Hot sparks flew. Nico leapt for the passageway's end just as the gun woman's body caught the electrical strike. A high-pitched male voice screamed, and in the white-lit passageway, the shadow of a male gnome briefly showed on the wall.

What the—? Nico landed and turned.

The dead gun woman hung suspended within the loudly buzzing electrical arc, her flesh burning. Nico neither heard nor saw any more from the gnome. She set her flowers safely aside from the rain of sparks, and then peered more into the lit passageway.

A side-flash branched from the gun woman's body and struck Nico.

Nico's muscles seized. Her back slammed into the wall. She slid down as the gun woman's smoking body fell away. The bright electrical arc cut and the dead redhead's gloved hands dropped.

Somewhere in the darkened passageway, the gnome whimpered. Nico moved a pained finger and groaned. She hoped Dorothy was shielded properly. Her Id glass scrolled data, already rebooting.

Nico swallowed. "Hey gnome, are you dying? Where are you? I can't help if you stay in the faerie realm."

"I'm here, here," a little male voice cried piteously.

Nico moved her head in the direction of the voice, located somewhere behind the redhead's body.

Her Id glass flashed.

Faerie kind detected: Leprechaun. Treasure hoarder, prankster, shoe-maker. Favours solitude. May be dressed in a red or green coat with hat and finery. Will offer three wishes when captured.

A trembling little man in a green coat and a cocked hat, standing no more than ten inches high, hugged the wall. Half his face was burnt and the blistered eye shut, but his suffering didn't diminish the craggy lines of his face that made him look sly. At his feet was a sack, bulging with coin-shaped objects. The dead redhead's body blocked him from escape.

Nico dropped her gaze to the redhead's busty chest. Her medals were missing.

"Where? I can't see you," Nico called.

"Over here," the leprechaun cried.

His shape and colours became sharply defined to her Id glass.

Leprechaun, de-cloaking, her Id glass gave.

"There you are," Nico said, staring directly at the little man. "Hate to tell you this, but you're screwed."

"Help me," the leprechaun shrieked.

Nico forced her limbs to move. Slowly, she undid the knot of her necktie.

After crawling to a position outside the passageway and close to the dead redhead, Nico tossed the end of her tie to the leprechaun. He took firm hold, his sack on his back. She pulled.

He flew up and over the redhead, her gloved hands jerking up. The electrical arc erupted into bright illumination as he cleared the woman's body.

Nico snatched him out of the air. Her grip tightened as the redhead's hands deactivated and dropped again, sparks falling.

"Hi. I lied. I can't help you," Nico said.

"I'm just a poor gnome," the leprechaun squealed. "Please don't hurt me."

"You're a gnome all right, all cheery-faced and friendly with a gnome wife somewhere. Why so far from home, gnome?" Nico demanded. "What kind of lowlife boss makes you loot bodies?"

"She does no such thing!"

"Oh? Well, your boss has been glamour-bombing since she got here. Is she so scared to walk openly among us?"

"Ya leave our princess alone," the leprechaun hollered. He grabbed for Nico's Damara Airship button.

"*Hey.*" Nico pulled him away before he could snatch it.

A sly look entered his face. "I'll grant ye three wishes."

"No thanks. What does your princess wa—"

Nico's fangs broke out as the leprechaun sank a throwing knife into the back of her hand. She dropped him and he pulled out a second knife, stabbing her through her resting hand and pinning it to the floor.

"You *little*—" Nico yelled.

"*Die, bloodsucker,*" he screeched and ran swiftly for the wrapped flowers on the floor.

"Don't touch Heloise's—"

Nico bit on the blade handle in her free hand and pulled it out. She grabbed it from her mouth and threw.

The leprechaun shrieked, the blade clipping his arm. He dropped the wrapped roses and ran wailing down the connecting corridor. He blipped from view once out of range of her Id glass.

"I will *bite* your head off if I see you again," Nico shouted after him.

I should have killed that little—but I don't know what the consequences are if I did murder him.

She looked at her stabbed hands, trembling with pain. With her veins dead, blood oozed rather than squirted.

"We're going to need three pints after this," she ground out to Bear and plucked out the blade handle in her pinned hand.

After willing her throbbing hands to hurry up and heal, she gingerly fetched her Id. To her relief, Dorothy was undamaged.

I found out who the higher faerie is. It's one female, Nico shakily typed to Shayla. *Might be a princess.* She rose and retrieved her black marker.

Shayla answered while Nico was taking photos of the passageway after writing a big warning on the floor.

Shayla: *Thank you, Love, and how did you find that out?*

"Erm," Nico said.

Nico: *A leprechaun told me?*

Shayla: *Did he try to kill you?*

"Um," Nico said.

Shayla: *Ya naughty lass. I'm waiting for security to let me in when the evacuees clear. Come to me when it's safe.*

Nico: *I love you.*

She then sent the photos and a brief message to Gimel's security and the Makepeace hotline.

After retying her necktie and straightening her blood encrusted outfit and Bear, she retrieved her flowers and followed the corridor marked: *This way to G-Gates 47 to 21.*

CHAPTER SIX

Gate 45—Gate 43— 42—

The thirteen gates Nico passed were deserted.

The spacious waiting areas were well designed, with reflective surfaces that made the section seem bigger than it was. She passed glass-enclosed art exhibits, entertainment holo stations, and sleep cubes. A section with such amenities was certain to have vibronic showers.

Nico shook out her dominant hand. Both her hands and stabbed side ached, her bloodied clothing looking like she'd recently murdered someone. She needed to clean up before greeting Heloise.

Her Id glass spotted no leprechaun or fae. An inactive security bot or android gate attendant stood about in silence, but there were no bodies present, and no damage. The section was simply abandoned.

She nearly wanted to give a thumbs up to any camera that might be working and acknowledge a seemingly successful evacuation. As she passed Gate 38, her vampire's hearing picked up a heated argument behind the shielded boarding doors.

"I sense nothing wrong out there," a man's voice declared. "Not a living soul. If we can't evacuate to the airfield, we should get out through here."

"Sir, we're not allowed to leave yet. Once the incident is taken care of, which will be shortly, then we can disembark," another voice soothed.

"You keep saying that, but we're still here, and I tell you, no one's in the waiting area," the man said. "Except some vampire."

Nico paused in her perusal of the arrivals holo-board. She turned around and gaped at the shut gate.

"I don't believe in psychics," she yelled at it.

"Oh yeah? Well it's some vampire," the man loudly added, "carrying *roses*."

Nico gaped more.

"What are you doing out there with those, anyway?" the man called. "Looking for trouble?"

"Mentalist," Nico accused, "you figure it out." Darque-world had its share of scam artists and performers professing true psionic ability. But this mentalist's guesses were too good.

When the argument resumed behind the shut doors, the psychic's ability then questioned, she snorted and returned her attention to the holo-board. Heloise's flight showed green for Gate 7.

"We should stop at a lavatory and take a quick vibronic shower," she told Bear. "Get all this blood out."

A woman screamed in the distance.

Nico took off with a vampire's speed and sped past

Gate 34.

In the next section, the boarding doors' shield for Gate 27 hung partially open. Travellers lay bloodied as if having succumbed to a beating. An overturned kiosk's snacks and bottles littered the corridor.

Two flight attendants wearing Id glasses protected the opening by swinging battered metal serving trays at crooked-faced little men with twisted, muscled bodies. The little men jeered and taunted.

Nico's Id glass flashed.

Faerie kind detected: Spriggans. Treasure thieves and faerie bodyguards. Bad weather and whirlwind makers; child stealers and crop blighters. Ability to swell to the size of giants.

"Dorothy, what will happen if I kill a faerie?" Nico demanded.

"Retribution by faerie kind includes eternal curses—"

"Okay, never mind."

She sped for the confrontation and punched three spriggans in succession.

"Why'd you let your passengers out?" Nico yelled at the flight attendants.

"We didn't," the steward answered, exasperated. "They somehow got the—"

"Behind you," the stewardess cried.

The steward spun and walloped a spriggan before it could reach the opened shield barrier.

"Both of you, get back to your plane," Nico ordered. "I'll shut the barrier."

"Not without our—" the stewardess said.

"I'll take care of it," Nico shouted. "Go!" She kicked a spriggan and sent him flying into three more of his companions.

Nico bit her flowers' wrapping and grabbed hold of the barrier's edge as the flight attendants scrambled beneath. She pushed down, the barrier creaking.

It's resisting. Whoever fiddled with it may've locked it in position.

Nico was strong enough to flip two-ton cars, but her brute strength barely budged the barrier. She felt it slowly inch back up.

What the—

The flight attendants shouted on the other side, their metal trays banging something below her. Nico looked down into the grinning face of a stout spriggan, wedged into the opening and holding the barrier up. He slowly swelled in size, raising the barrier higher.

Nico grabbed his nose and twisted.

The spriggan screamed and let go. Nico pulled hard on the spriggan's nose and flung him away. With a press of her arms, she brought the barrier down until it shut.

"*Help*," a woman screamed.

Nico spun.

Spriggans straddled a fallen woman's back and pulled at her greying hair.

"*Ah*," she shrieked.

Nico ran up as one laughing spriggan swelled, pinning the woman with his rapidly gaining weight. She hauled him up and punted him. More spriggans followed as Nico snatched them away from their victim, the actions jerking the woman's head.

"You horrible little vampire," the woman cried. "Stop pulling my hair!"

Nico removed the wrapped flowers from her mouth. "I wasn't pulling your hair, there were *spriggans* in it."

"W-what?" The woman looked around, baffled. The spriggans clung to columns and jeered, their long teeth sharp as the oblivious woman stared in their direction.

"Never mind. Back off," Nico shouted at the spriggans. "What's it going to take to make your princess leave everyone alone?"

One spriggan leapt, his club-like fists up.

"*Damara talisman*," he screamed, bringing a hand down for Nico's pin-back.

"Don't touch my *stuff*." Nico punched him.

Three spriggans raised their large hands and pointed at her. Nico threw her flowers aside.

A powerful wind spun at her feet and grabbed her body, sending her spiralling face first into the ceiling high above. She dented the panel with a loud bang. The whirlwind rattled Nico against the ceiling. When it died, she fell, hitting the floor with her backside.

Nico wiped blood from her nose as she stared with cracked lenses at the ceiling. The woman gaped at her.

"What are you *doing*?" she exclaimed. "Why did you fly up there?"

"I don't know how to fly," Nico said sourly. "Can't you hear the spriggans laughing?"

The woman stared as if Nico were crazy.

"Do you know what your problem is? Belief." Nico pointed at her. "Things like me will get you if you don't believe in us."

The laughing spriggans silenced, their ears pricking. They bounded away. Nico sprang up, grabbed her flowers, and ran after them, the faeries hopping swiftly out of range of her Id glasses' perception filter. They disappeared as their surroundings swallowed them up, a curtain dropping.

Nico slowed. She dusted off Bear.

Faerie bodyguards. That could only mean....

Something golden flashed at the corner of her eye. Nico whirled.

A figure's reflection—

Bone-white hair flowing—

The girl's golden skinned image flitted across the reflective panels of Gate 29, her distant and hollow laughter reverberating. Nico steadied her damaged frames and quickly tracked.

"Id glass, scan for faerie presence," she ordered.

No lower fae detected, her Id glass returned.

"I meant higher faerie." She continued to scan but knew the movement had travelled beyond her glasses' range. Her Id glass returned a negative.

The girl in the corridor's reflective surfaces was gone.

"Who were you talking to?" the woman called.

"My flowers," Nico snapped.

She checked the state of her roses.

Nico lifted the barrier for the flight attendants to reemerge. As they tended to the spriggans' victims, the steward mentioned getting the wounded cleared to the tarmac for emergency services.

"The tower told the captain. Help is coming," he said to Nico.

"Help is coming from the tarmac, not from behind us?" Nico indicated the sections she'd traversed. She still expected security and emergency services to access Gimel through Gate 84's section and progress from there.

"That's a good question. But however it's handled, Gimel will have this all cleaned up within the hour. A spaceport can't be shut down." The steward grinned. "This isn't as bad as when were-raptors on mescaline went after all the vampires in the 'port. Boy, was that a murder fest."

Nico cleared her throat.

"It's a good thing you weren't there," the stewardess chimed in, smiling.

While the flight attendants administered first aid to their errant passengers, Nico left. In her bloodstained condition, she preferred not risking detainment whenever help and the authorities deigned to appear.

She sent a message to Shayla, telling her of the spriggans and the golden girl.

Shayla: *Thank you, Love. I'm sorry that happened. The guild's faerie wranglers are here but we're still not allowed to enter.*

Nico: *Surely the security head will finally believe a bunch of mean little faeries took down Gimel? The flight attendants saw them. Or is he afraid the witches' guild will incur an eternal curse?*

Shayla: *Ya wound me, chick. Since when have I let something curse ya? And don't call me—*

"'Shirley,'" Nico quoted and guffawed. Shayla barely understood the later 20th century humour of the movie, Airplane! when Nico played it on her rescued VHS machine, but the "don't call me Shirley" routine had made Shayla laugh.

Shayla: *He prefers the Makepeace handle this, Love.*

"Xenophobe," Nico muttered to Bear. Even on Darqueworld, she'd encountered several of those.

Shayla: *Dinna enter the area of gates 1 to 20 until the Makepeace gives the all clear.*

Nico: *Ok.* She sent Shayla the song, "For Your Love."

Nico slowed in her walk, realising she'd reached Gate 21. Ahead, deserted shops came into view: gift shops, luxury goods, and leisure goods. Her cracked Id glass returned a negative for faerie presence.

"Why not?" she said to Bear and entered.

Gleaming storefronts of glass lined the corridor. Merchandise lay knocked over and scattered on the floors within. One shop, filled with high-end bags and accessories, had its glass entrance firmly sealed.

A rosy-cheeked porcelain doll with tumbling golden curls and a Cupid's bow mouth stood behind the locked entrance, wearing a shop clerk's uniform. Her head was as high as Nico's knee. Her glass blue eyes followed Nico's passage.

Nico made Bear wave at her, and then returned her attention to the corridor.

"Just keep walking," she murmured to Bear.

Fresh blood scented.

Nico's head turned, her nose following the faint smell. It drifted from a shut bathroom facility—one frightened travellers or shop workers might hide barricaded behind.

Nico paused, debating her need for a shower or to have her stained hands washed, at least.

Let's not disturb them, she thought to Bear. *We might get a fire extinguisher sprayed in the face for our trouble.*

A postcard spinning rack creaked, drawing Nico's attention.

The rack slowly spun. Behind it, a security bot stood, its holo bulletin flashing.

MIND MIND MIND MIND MIND, it read.

Wheels whirled behind her, fast approaching.

Nico leapt aside and flattened against a newsstand. A security bot hurtled down the corridor, blackened by electrical attack. Little brown men rode the bot.

It sped down the corridor and sent the magazines at Nico's feet rustling. The bot disappeared into the next section.

Nico looked down at the strewn magazines and picked up one glossy: the *New Times*. Its cover of Damara Airship was torn off. All the *New Times* copies at her feet lacked covers.

Faerie laughter sounded, far ahead, and the low pulse of a Makepeace's weapon, firing. Nico listened and marked the sounds' distance; the confrontation was only a few seconds away.

She checked Dorothy. Heloise would arrive in ten minutes. Silence fell.

Nico stood, flowers in hand.

"We could look for another lavatory," she suggested to Bear. "Or one of those amenities stations. One with a mender for the slash in my clothes." She examined the damage, her fingers poking through the knife slice.

Her gaze drifted in the pressing silence.

"Never mind," she exhaled. "Let's screw this up."

She ran into a luxury sporting goods shop.

"A hammer, a horseshoe, a tire iron?" she queried aloud. A bag of golf clubs stood in the window.

She tossed golf irons. "Aluminium, titanium—aluminium, zinc—"

"There's no such thing as real golf *irons*," she exclaimed to Bear. She ran across to the snacks and gifts shop.

"Bread, butter—milk—real bread, please?" She searched through all the wrapped and boxed foods. She considered a package of sealed snack cake. Then she saw the refrigerated display, stocked with selected craft brews and ready for insulated gift boxes.

She grabbed two dark bottles of Irish stout from the unit and scanned her credit chit at the counter.

Dorothy pinged. Nico pulled her Id out.

Heloise: *I can see Again NewYork. See you soon.*

Nico sent her the song, "Heart Full Of Soul," and then ran out of the store for the corridor marked: *This way to G-Gates 20 to 01.*

CHAPTER SEVEN

Nico set foot in the silent area of G-Gates 20 through 1, seeing no one. Paper whirled in the distance, a tiny tornado spinning in the corridor's midst. She sidestepped away from the corridor proper and hid behind a column.

The little tornado spun, the glossy paper flashing.

"Id glass, who's making that whirlwind?" Nico whispered.

Targeted area is beyond perception range, her Id glass gave, flashing a negative.

Nico advanced slowly from column to column, silent as a ghost.

Gate 12…11….

She pressed against The Wing lounge's wall and slid against its polished marble, blending herself and Bear with the black surface. Her Id glass continued to return a negative as she neared the whirlwind. A familiar image became apparent on the flying, torn glossies: Damara Airship.

Nico glanced down. Before the rustling *New Times* covers, a Makepeace's armoured boot and leg rested in the corridor, the rest of the body obscured by a column.

Nico slipped behind another column. The frantic flapping of paper continued.

"Id glass, optimise Second Sight for higher fae," she whispered.

Id glass: *Optimising.*

The whirlwind drifted away, slowly progressing down the corridor for Gate 1.

No faerie kind detected, her Id glass gave.

Nico swallowed. She could not smell it—hear it, taste it—but something...*someone* still felt present. She stared again.

I believe. Show me.

Her Id glass continued to flash a negative.

She glanced aside at the gate area she hid in: Gate 7. The sunlit tarmac outside showed no ship at the boarding doors.

Nico returned her attention to the Makepeace's foot lying ahead and crept forwards, the retreating covers wildly dancing. She stepped over a helm that had been tossed aside and rounded the column.

A bareheaded Makepeace sat with his back propped. She recognised his mouth.

Nico slowly knelt as Nick's silver-eyed gaze followed her.

"E—vac—vac—citizen," Nick uttered.

"I will," Nico whispered. She set one of the ale bottles before him. Putting her flowers aside, she gripped the bottle's perspiring neck.

She pulled the cap off, its toothy edge tearing her fingertips. Beer foam coated. She moved back as the scent of smoky ale permeated.

Brown dots rushed from beneath Nick's armour and down his body for the bottle's spout. The little men did not bother to enlarge but dove in. Even through the dark glass, Nico could discern the liquid reducing.

She returned her attention to the Makepeace. Nick's gaze lay above her shoulder, watching.

What—?

The flutter of paper grew louder.

Before she could turn, brown dots leapt from the bottle for Mr Bear.

Nico scrambled back, the minuscule brownies disappearing behind Bear.

Oh gods—

Nico froze, waiting for the bite of tiny axes.

"Warning," Dorothy emitted and fell silent.

The opening guitar strains of "Ten Miles High" began.

The volume rose.

Nico turned as wind caught her hair. The tornado spun beside her, the *New Times* covers slapping. Their spin widened—parted to reveal the tornado's eye. Nico's song deafened and enveloped as she stared within the whirlwind.

Bone-white hair flew, wild, and a girl's bare back, golden-skinned and glowing, pulsed with luminescent, dark tattoos. Her worn denim jeans hung low, revealing the top of her intergluteal cleft. The bell-bottomed legs were pinned with Damara Airship buttons. The magazine covers scattered away.

Nico's lenses flashed.

Faerie kind detected: level Aos Sí.

The faerie girl turned to Nico, her hair settling over shiny, little breasts.

Multi-coloured irises like kaleidoscopes; black-diamond pupils that glittered. Her golden cheeks were streaked with sparkling moisture. The faerie girl's pink, dewy mouth stretched in a manic smile, tiny teeth nibbling on a red mushroom cap. The Dragon's Eye of Damara Airship decorated her shining belly, painted in purple.

Add on Glamour Annihilator, Nico's Id glass interrupted, *for true perception of the faerie kind.*

Nico swallowed.

I....

I don't think I want to see what's under this glamour.

Sprites giggled and darted in the air and around the girl's bare feet. Three flew for Nico's face.

They snatched at Nico's damaged cat's eye frames and snapped it at the bridge. The right side of her frames caught on her ear. The three flew away with half of her Id glass in their grip.

An empty corridor showed to Nico's left eye, and a golden girl with floating hair in her other. Nico grabbed for her flowers and the second bottle of stout. She wrested the bottle cap off and held the opened bottle out.

The faerie's glistening lips parted and laughter issued, hollow and high.

Froth shot up from the bottle's spout and showered. Nico blinked beer from her eyes as the winged fae shrieked in mirth. The faerie girl reached for Nico, her long, white fingernails like filed bone.

The cold fingers wrapped around the bottle's neck and Nico's hand and didn't let go.

Leaves rustled in Nico's ears; cool wind touched her skin. The scent of pungent earth, mossy and wet, hit her tongue and filled her nostrils and dead lungs.

Gem facets rotated in the faerie girl's shining eyes.

Warning, Nico's beer-streaked lens gave. *You have been abducted into the faerie realm. Warning—*

The faerie's pink lips moved.

DA MARA—

The wind, the trees, the grass, the sky said—

AIRSHIP?

Nico's lips parted to speak. She tasted ale. Her line of sight seemed to fall—tilt. She was far below the faerie's gem faceted eyes—

I'm shrinking?

No; she was sinking. A bog trapped her, surrounding her vision with rainbow soap bubbles. Submerged in that quicksand, she might become a desiccated mummy, a sunken gold trinket. A forgotten object, left behind in the faerie realm by the faerie girl if Nico did not speak.

"They're—" Nico's voice was fingernails rubbing loudly against helium balloons. "Damara Airship is not here. If you want to—"

TWO? the girl said.

"—to *see* them, you'll need tickets."

The faerie nibbled on rose petals. Her words sank into Nico's soap bubble head.

TIC, Kets?

Tickets, Nico tried to say. *Admission, to see them—play—*

Nico searched for her mouth.

The faerie touched the Damara Airship pin-back on Nico's chest.

Her golden hand drew back like one burnt. Darkness engulfed and her eyes lit, cold and sharp shards.

The gaze disappeared, replaced by kaleidoscoping eyes.

The faerie ate more rose petals.

YOU—

Her dewy mouth said.

GIVE us—

TIC, Kets—

"I can't," Nico said with Bear's voice. Bear was still Bear, wasn't he? Nico was a drowning mushroom, the faerie atop and smothering her. Rose petals fell on Nico's once-face. She was under peat and bog water, under masses of swirling flowers, sinking.

I'm dead already...I cannot drown.

"But I know someone," Nico/Bear said, word bubbles rising and popping. The psychedelic guitars of "Ten Miles High" swirled with her.

The faerie smiled, her lips stretching over many, tiny teeth.

"Follow." Nico made Bear point to the gently glowing exit arrows in the soaked moss, uncertain if her limbs were wiggly roots, waving branches—undulating grass-hair. "The witch is waiting for you."

Laughter dropped from the girl's pink lips like gem shards, hitting Nico in the face. The kaleidoscope eyes lifted.

The faerie girl split into two.

Whaaa?

But Nico happened to face the direction of the faerie girl's departure—or perhaps the faerie girl had let Nico go, allowing her head to loll that way—and witnessed only one of the girl through her cracked Id glass, the lower fae flitting and hopping after. The faerie's moving bottom and fluttering bone-white hair shimmered. Her shape trembled into fading gold, then disappeared from Nico's perception filter.

The miasma that was Nico's head lifted, a thunderhead ascending.

Nico sat up. She smelled carpeting, vinyl seats, recycled air. No wind blew; no bog water clogged her dead lungs. Moisture streaked her own cheeks, whether from beer or her own tears, she did not know. She was alone with Nick at Gate 7 while the Avians sang.

When she looked down, her hands clutched crumpled, green wrapping. Flower stems lay scattered in the corridor leading towards Gate 1, the heads eaten.

Nico screamed in horror.

CHAPTER EIGHT

Shayla frowned and deactivated her Id ring. Nico's Id was bouncing back attempts to contact it. The Makepeace sent in to deal with the coming *Aos Sí* was taking too long, and she wanted Niky to know.

When she looked about the terminal arcade she stood in, her vision eerily hazed, perceiving more colours in her environment than were present to the mundane eye. She resisted passing her hand before her eyes to correct it. The visual experience from conjured second sight was not comfortable for her.

She walked towards the line of security personnel manning a tape barrier, erected before the passageway leading to the eighty-eight boarding gates. Eateries lined the arcade before the demarcation. The little shops were filled with gawkers, the lingering evacuees—waiting for their opportunity to return—and to her chagrin, droves of loitering Damara

Airship fans, holding handmade signs and items for auto-
graphing. Somehow, Shawn and the band's true arrival gate
at Gimel had been discovered.

Shayla ignored the kids since they hadn't guessed who she
was yet. Her fellow guild members, all faerie wranglers, waited patiently near the tape with their tools in hand. Shayla
came to stand before the busy security head.

The wiry man was obviously Old Earth ex-military or police and apparently good at his job, but he was no longtime
resident of Darqueworld, as Shayla discovered. She knew
from serving pie and coffee to countless chrono-arrivals at
Lucy's that if newcomers could not accept certain realities,
nothing would convince them otherwise. And she preferred
that the security head did not learn the hard way of the true
existence of invisible wee folk and the very real harm they
wrought. He was not only responsible for himself, after all,
but for everyone in Gimel.

The man regarded her.

"You again?" he said, incredulous. "Didn't I have you es-
corted away?"

"It's time ye let the wranglers go in," Shayla stated.

"Get this young woman out of my sight," the security head
demanded, gesturing to a female officer, but Shayla held up a
hand to the woman reaching for her.

"Ye lost three Makepeace tae the *Aos Sí* already and would
sacrifice more? What will the city say tae that? Or the under-
holarchy?" Shayla demanded.

"That's enough," the security head threatened. Excitement
suddenly stirred along the line, and the man spun to see what
the commotion was about.

A great cloud bloomed from the passageway and expanded
into the arcade, the sparkling mass emitting lights, colours,

and floating bubbles. The mass quickly swelled.

Thunderhead, Shayla grimly thought.

"It's a psychedelic trick," the security head barked. "Keep watch for who's hidden in it."

"There!" someone shouted.

A golden girl—with flowing white hair and an otherworldly glow—glided ghostlike within the sparkling cloud. As she walked, she laughed and tilted a dark bottle to her lips. Then she shimmered from perception, slipping between the veils of reality.

"Some kind of chameleon Other-being," the security head called out. "She's camouflaged—scan for her body temps!"

"That won't work when the *Aos Sí*'s in her realm. She's coming towards ye lot *right now*," Shayla warned.

"And how do you know that? You said you don't have the 'sight,'" the security head accused, sarcastic.

Shayla ignored him. The *Aos Sí*'s tinier kin barrelled through the thunderhead, laughing and squealing. Shayla focused her gaze upon the advancing cloud and raised a hand. She activated weird matter above it.

A weird matter explosion erupted above the thunderhead, bursting it apart. Shockwaves rippled, wiping out sparkling motes and rainbow bubbles in its wake. Pixies tumbled through the air while wranglers swung nets to catch them. The people before the tape stumbled back, pushed down by the shockwave's force.

"What—the hell?" the security head uttered.

"They're coming," Shayla said. She turned to mark the *Aos Sí*'s passage through the line of security as spriggans hooted and shrieked, jumping upon the confused humans before them. A one-sided fight ensued as people fell beneath clobbering, invisible fists. Brownies burst from the passageway on a commandeered security bot.

"Sook-sook-sook," a witch called, and laid a milk pail down. The brownies crashed the bot to the floor and skidded to a stop. They swarmed from the bot for the milk.

Shayla watched as the faerie girl entered an ice cream and confections parlour with a Shawn O'Fey poster hung in the window. Flying sprites followed, playing catch with something that looked familiar.

Shayla pushed through the bewildered security officers. Spriggans hopped into her path and raised fists.

"You, *aside*. Ya stand aside, right *now*," Shayla ordered, sweeping her hand.

Agape, the spriggans halted.

Shayla walked determinedly into the parlour.

Nico ran, tapping on Dorothy's activation button. "Ten Miles High" had finally stopped playing, but her Id refused to wake up.

"C'mon, I need to tell Shayla that the faerie girl wants Shawn's baby. Or give him a blow job, either way," she said in aside to Bear.

Repairing, Dorothy's surface then said.

Nico put her Id away as she exited the passageway into Gimel's arcade. She ran up to a torn and tangled tape barrier and vaulted over the beleaguered security personnel being beaten up by spriggans. The crackling scent of weird matter discharge hit her nostrils.

That's Shayla's work—

Nico landed and punched a spriggan. A bearded man in braids grabbed another and thrust the screaming faerie into a large, wiggling sack. Nico searched through the people and confusion, unable to mark Shayla's perfumed scent.

A flower seller shouted. Nico's Id glass recognised more spriggans, gleefully scattering bouquets to the ground. The seller vainly pressed against a glass fridge door holding his best flower arrangements, keeping it shut against the assailants who snatched at the door handle and jeered.

"Ghosts," the flower seller yelled. "Genii! *Demons!* Help!"

Nico searched for a weapon. At one eatery, a cook stood looking on, an iron skillet and spatula in hand.

She ran up and snatched the skillet. "I need that. Thank you," she said to the startled cook. Then she sped for the flower stand and swung.

BANG—BANG—

The spriggans howled and clutched their heads, their skin sizzling where the iron had touched. They hopped madly away, and Nico flung the pan.

It skimmed the heads of three spriggans in succession, bowling them over.

"And don't come back," Nico yelled. She turned to the flower seller. "Okay, your demons are gone."

"Oh, thank the gods—"

"Don't thank them, thank *me*." Nico produced her credit chit. "Sell me those roses in the fridge unit, *now*."

Nick the Makepeace had emerged from Gimel's passageway when Nico ran back, apparently recovered from the brownies attack. The fact that he appeared undamaged seemed to assure everyone present that all was clear. Either that or the impatient travellers and loiterers took it upon themselves to breach the downed tape barrier and retake Gimel.

While the security head yelled for everyone to stop, Nico raced with the rest, outpacing the frantic Damara Airship fans running with their signs. She ducked into a vibronic shower facility next to the bathrooms at Gate 4 and scanned her credit chit.

"Hurry-hurry," Nico said, as the vibrations removed the particles of beer and blood from her clothes and hair. The ale streaks disappeared from her one lens.

Next to her, a bloodied and weary traveller helped another mend a scrape at the first aid station. The two stared at Nico fearfully.

"I did not murder anyone today," Nico protested. "Take my photo! Send it to the police! I have to meet my lover!"

When the couple chose not to take her holo-snap, Nico grabbed her new flowers and leapt from the shower. She re-entered the swelling crowd. A ship slowly docked at the boarding doors of Gate 7. Dorothy pinged.

"Good, you're working again." Nico pulled her Id out.

Where are you, Shayla's message said, the urgent words flashing. Nico quickly typed.

At Heloise's gate. I'm okay. She gave Shayla the gate number.

Shayla: *Sprites had half yr frames all broke—*

Your Id kept gieing back an error—

Ye gied me a fright *Lass—*

Nico: *I'm sorry I'm ok I'm so sorry*.

Shayla: *I'm with the* Aos Sí. *She agreed to be peaceful if I gie her our new tickets, Love. I had no good reason to refuse her.*

Nico: *I understand. Don't worry. It's ok*. She had put the burden of placating the faerie girl on Shayla, after all.

Shayla: *I'll join you two soon.*

Nico sent her the song, "Ten Miles High."

✈

At Gate 7, Nico hastily removed her broken lens, pocketed it, and tried to order her disheveled hair before a column's reflective surface. She then straightened her tie and Bear. Once done, she quickly faced the boarding doors, flowers in hand, as they slowly opened.

She took on the aspect she'd meant to present at Gate 84, of a calm and smiling Nico who'd never heard of much less met any terrorising faerie folk. Tired and rumpled travellers issued from the doors. She didn't have to wait long for a tall and dark-haired woman to appear.

A Beckensdale trench coat thrown over a business suit; a skirt cut high enough to show off shapely legs—Heloise Allen sauntered through the doors as if she owned the ship she'd departed, her confident regard exhibiting no fatigue from her extended journey. Her stiletto heels clicked as she put a cigarette to her smiling red lips, her blue-eyed and sardonic gaze resting on Nico. A human gate attendant approached.

"Ms—"

"Madame," Heloise corrected.

"Ma'am, you can't light that here," he said apologetically.

Heloise ignored him. She smirked at Nico as she neared, her unlit cigarette dangling.

"Baby," she said.

Nico met her and pulled the cigarette from Heloise's mouth. She went to tiptoe to kiss her.

When their kiss ended, Nico gave her the roses.

"Doll, they're beautiful," Heloise enthused. She brought the roses to her nose and inhaled. "Mmm. And so pink."

"I—they ran out of red ones." Nico nervously put the cigarette behind her ear. "You should have seen—sometimes faeries come by and bite the heads off. At least these are perfect."

Heloise grinned, mirthful. "Did you punch out some of the little folk?"

"I did."

"That's my girl. Well, by the looks of this crowd, the fae incursion must be over. Thank you for keeping my flowers safe."

"Mm," Nico said, looking aside. Heloise sniffed Nico's hair.

Her sharp brow rose. Heloise then looked down, noticing the neat tear in Nico's cardigan. She poked through it and the slit shirt beneath, brushing skin.

"That *tickles*," Nico said, embarrassed, and pulled away.

A departing female passenger gave them a droll look as Heloise's mouth parted to form a question.

"Enjoy," she bade, smiling at Heloise.

"Thank you," Heloise answered, grinning. She hugged Nico to her as the woman walked away. "We will."

"That was rude," Nico declared.

"She wasn't talking about you, sweetheart," Heloise soothed. "Hey, I've a surprise."

Nico eagerly frisked her, searching for the lolly.

"Wh-whoa—wait." Heloise extricated herself and activated the steel Id ring on her middle finger.

Three Damara Airship concert tickets holo-projected. Heloise indicated the departing woman.

"She works publicity for Damara Airship." Heloise deactivated her ring and leaned in to whisper. "I didn't exactly say I was sleeping with the lead singer's sister, but she got the idea." She sniffed Nico's hair again. "Why do you smell like ozone…and beer?"

"Oh," Nico hurriedly said. She waved, dismissive. "I was hit by lightning. And…some people are just so rude. Thank you for getting the tickets," she added gratefully. "You know, if you'd chosen to fly on a Wayra ship, you could have arrived with the band."

"Really? Wouldn't that have been a tight fit with those love-ly, long-legged boys. I've looked at Wayra ships—too narrow. They remind me of how claustrophobic Concordes were." Heloise's gaze then snapped up as if she heard something, and Nico looked to where she focused.

Shayla pushed urgently through the noisy crowd, two hundred feet away. She shouted something only Heloise's elder vampire's hearing could catch. Nico watched Shayla's mouth move.

Doppelgänger, Shayla's lips said. *She's still HERE—*

"The faerie girl," Nico ejected. She pulled out her remaining lens and left Heloise to run for Gate 10.

"I need this. Thank you." Nico snatched a green bottle of mineral water from the ice laid out in a beverages cart and tossed the attendant her credit chit. Heloise stood in perplex-ity, having shadowed Nico with an elder vampire's swift ease. Nico pushed through the Damara Airship fans watching Gate 10's roped off and closed arrival doors. She searched the area with her cracked Id glass.

"Id glass, scan for—"

Higher faerie detected, her Id glass returned. The faerie girl of flowing bone-white hair and glowing skin stood at the ropes nearest the doors, her bare back to Nico. Sprites hovered above her. The fans gathered near seemed oblivious to her presence.

The arrival doors swung open.

The Wayra's passengers flooded out of the doors and filled the roped area.

"Is the faerie girl real now—in our reality now? Tell me," Nico demanded from her Id glass.

Faerie de-cloaking, her Id glass gave. The faerie girl's body gained sharp definition before Nico's Id-vision as a phalanx of wary bodyguards exited Gate 10's departure doors. The girl raised her hand, sparkling motes building.

Nico flung the bottle.

It flew, end over end, high over the heads of the waiting area crowd. Its falling arc ended on the faerie girl's head with a loud crack. She hit the floor like a felled tree.

"That's for eating my flowers," Nico yelled.

Shayla ran up. Once through the confused crowd and by the faerie girl's side, Shayla spoke a spell of binding and bound the girl with the red ribbon she'd intended for Heloise.

Alarmed bystanders, realising the true nature of the rousing victim, backed away. The bodyguards blocked their charges from proceeding out the boarding doors.

An unearthly scream rose from the bound faerie girl, and Shayla pointed at her.

"Stitch it, devil's darning needles," she commanded, and the girl's noise abruptly ceased.

Even in her waitress's uniform and corduroy coat,   Shayla exuded the authority of a coven's gunslinger. Her raised hands and angry gaze encapsulated all the invisible fae who huddled or fluttered around their fallen mistress. In a hushed gate area, she named all the little folk and formally admonished them, her words fiery.

Nico shrank with the crowd at the severe chastisement.

She did have to leave work to deal with this.

"Beautiful throw, baby," Heloise said behind her.

Nico looked up. Heloise watched the area around Shayla with her own pair of frameless Id-wear. "She should hurry with that admonition so her brother can come out. Oh— here we go," she added wryly. "Boys always know when to interrupt."

Shawn O'Fey pushed past his bodyguards and flung the rope barrier aside. He pulled Shayla into a hug, halting her in mid-sentence. The fans screamed.

Heloise gave her flowers to the cart attendant as the fans surged forwards.

WHOMP—

Weird matter energy exploded above Shayla, the shockwave pushing the fans back, but Nico knew Shayla couldn't pull the trick again without hurting someone. She grinned up at Heloise.

"Time to get her and leave?" Heloise said.

"It is. Let's screw this up."

They jumped into the crowd.

The events of *Fae Came On the Plane!* occur after *Monster Stalker* Volume 1 and *Bloody Nike* Volume 2.

PREVIEW:
MONSTER STALKER

Kill first.

CHAPTER ONE :

NOW ARRIVING

NICO was a bullet, piercing matter. She burst into dusky skies, an airfield fast approaching her face. She hit it and rolled.

Sun! Clouds shrouded it, but she felt its heat. She scrambled on the tarmac and saw no earth to bury herself in. When she didn't catch fire, she touched the black surface she knelt on, warmed by sunlight. Her free hand clutched her switchblade, its blade triggered. The hot handle sparked with electricity.

"Ow—ow," Nico said. She dropped her blade, pulled down her cardigan's sleeve over her burnt palm, then picked the knife up again.

Airfield? Buildings stood on the hazy horizon. She needed to run for cover. When she tried to stand, she plopped back instead. The airfield tilted as she fought nausea.

Mr. Bear, her sandy-coloured stuffed bear, sat strapped to the front of her black cardigan and white button-down. Nico looked down at the chest harness, made of leather, silver grommets, and fastenings, and could not remember purchasing it, much less donning it. Her left knee throbbed, and she raised it to look.

Beneath her short black skirt with the two pleats, her black stocking had torn at the knee; the bloodied bruise already healing from where she'd scraped it on landing. She had no memory of choosing her clothes or her shoes (which were the spike-studded leather oxfords and not her black Mary Janes) though it was an outfit she wore often.

A man in uniform coveralls and a ball cap with the logo *Jifk* walked across the airfield towards her. Somehow, she'd missed his approach. His tattooed face appeared friendly, and Nico thought his markings looked Maori. An identification badge dangled from his breast pocket: *Tane.*

Nico blinked. She'd read that in Cyrillic, but then it rearranged itself into the Latin alphabet.

"Here's another one," he said to no one in particular, though Nico couldn't be certain he spoke to someone via a mic. "Hey there. Can you put that away, please?" Nico looked at her blade, then shut it. "Thanks. Welcome to Again NewYork. I'm going to ask you to step over here and stand in that circle, and we'll get you processed right away." He brought up a rectangular-shaped device in his hand. "What's your name?"

"A—Again, New York?" Nico said.

"No, really. That's your name?" He indicated again that she move towards a circle blacker than the tarmac it lay in. She hadn't noticed it during her scrambling.

Nico tucked her switchblade into her skirt's waistband in back and rose. She stumbled to her feet, woozy. "No, I'm Nico," she said. "Nicolette Alexikova." Adrenaline receding, she felt a little like she'd been struck by lightning; her hair rose from static electricity. She looked at the pitch-black circle that resembled a pit, then at Tane. "Why am I—am I going to—?"

"Nope. You won't." Tane answered. Nico toed the blackness; it felt solid. "Both feet, please," Tane added. She put both feet into the circle.

Everything flashed, and she threw up her arms. When she looked down at herself and Bear, they were still in one piece.

"Vampire, right?" Tane touched his pad.

Nico froze.

"Well, your bio-dats say you are," Tane said. "And boy, did you get skittish when you saw you were in daylight."

Nico gave her surroundings a furtive look. "Again...New York?"

"Right." Tane continued to enter data. "Your teddy bear doesn't appear to be alive or sentient, so that's just one to process for immigration. Can you confirm that you're a vampire, please?"

"Yes. Yes I am," she said bravely. "And I've dual citizenship—American and British."

Tane looked up and grinned. "If that matters to you. But on Darqueworld, designations like that don't exist; the city-states are only what the gods make of them."

Darkworld? Nico tried to look closer at his badge. Electricity buzzed along her skin, and the air exploded, popping her ears. She ducked and looked behind her. Farther down the field, the atmosphere split. It erupted in fire and ejected a flaming man, the ends of his trench coat trailing. He tumbled on the ground and flopped to a stop. The hole sucked in upon itself and disappeared.

"Wow, what an entry—right out of an explosion." Tane's tone was matter-of-fact. Two bulky men blipped into view, and Nico blinked, thinking they'd stepped on to the tarmac as if from an invisible place. The men ran up to the one smoking on the ground—at least, Nico thought the two were men. Like Tane, they wore coveralls, but horns grew out of their heads, and their features had snouts and brows like bulls. Nico turned to Tane.

"Am I in purgatory?" she said.

Tane scrutinised her. "Don't know how you got here, huh? Memory loss." He entered something into his pad. "Don't worry, they'll have a Po get a good look at you, then assign you a social worker—"

"Social worker? *Now* I believe in hell."

"Oh, is that what you think this is?" Tane's tone was light.

"No...hell is getting murdered and stuff." Nico tried to ignore the sound of the two horned guys scraping the smoking fellow off the ground.

"It sure is. Hey," he said, catching her attention. "You're a chrono-immigrant, if that info helps—" He pointed at his head. "Jog your memory some. You took a trip to a planet settled by others like yourself, and here you are. I only need you to tell me your era. I'm betting it's late twentieth century."

Nico looked at him blankly. "The year is 1998."

"Great. Now, if you'll show me the back of your hand." He pulled out a device resembling a tattoo gun.

"What's that?" she said, wary.

"A biometric tagger." Tane motioned for her hand. Nico presented the back of her left hand, wondering if she was about to receive a barcode tattoo. Tane placed the tagger over her skin. A beam burst, pricking her. It felt like an inoculation. Then she remembered that as a vampire, she had no fear of diseases. The sensation ran up her wrist after Tane lifted the tagger, and she shook her hand, trying to rid herself of the tickle.

If I'm in a coma somewhere, someone just did something funny to my hand.

She wasn't certain if vampires could fall into actual comas, and dismissed that speculation. Tane gestured to a metal arch that Nico hadn't noticed before.

"All done! Enter that gate there, and you'll be processed and ready to start your new life in Again NewYork."

★

Chrono-immigrant? Nico approached the gate. It showed only the airfield beyond it. If everything happening was her conscious reality, perhaps the forethought of strapping Mr Bear to herself made sense. But what situation had she come out of, especially with blade drawn? Nico looked down in case she'd missed signs of violence on her person or clothes. She did not seek fights, but evil could follow a girl, as she well knew. If she'd been in danger in Leningrad before coming to...Again, New York, she couldn't recall what had happened or why.

Therefore, I was kidnapped somehow, and now I'm in some rich man's fantasy set. Or this is some crazy KGB plot to get vampires to out themselves.

She stepped through the gate.

And found herself in a security area aglow in dim blue, one with bored officers standing by roped-off stations and machines. None of the officers looked human, though humanoid enough. A great, glass bubble hung in the room's centre; inside a large, bald female head floated. She looked at Nico.

I'll ignore that. Nico stared instead at a pedestal sign with an illustration of a bald person's head in a bubble, accompanied by possibly important information. Nico couldn't read the language, so she returned her attention to the room.

A quick scan (while avoiding the staring head) seemed to affirm that she was the lone chrono-immigrant present. She hoped no one would confiscate her switchblade—Tane had not seemed to mind her carrying it. Nico checked her hand, not wanting an injury to delay processing. Thanks to a vampire's healing ability, the burn was gone and her skin, whole. She approached the nearest station, where a blue humanoid male looked down at her, impassive. On the counter sat a mounted tagger like the one Tane had used, and a large metal orb with a glass top. The blue male held up a lens.

The lens flashed, making Nico see colours, and the back of her hand itched.

"*Raqa*," he said, indicating the mounted tagger.

"You want my hand, right?" Nico said, and then noticed what the orb contained. An insect as large as a rat sat within, wearing a tiny badge. It waved feelers and seemed to look at her with its multi-faceted eyes.

"*Click-click,*" it said, its mandibles moving. Nico thrust her hand beneath the tagger, suppressing the urge to wallop the bug and run away. Rising in a shallow forest grave with beetles living in her mouth had not endeared her to insects. The bug pressed something on its tiny console.

The beam that hit her hand seared, but Nico saw no burn on her skin. She shook her hand again.

"Read that, please," the insect said motioning to its glass hatch, and Nico started in surprise. She was certain it had made more clicking sounds. A message illuminated across the orb's glass. Hieroglyphics rearranged, forming the Latin alphabet.

"*Hi farhol mal haro sowo,*" she read, bewildered. The insect's mouth clicked more, and the blue humanoid appeared to guffaw, as if they were sharing a laugh. Nico gave them a look, hoping they hadn't made her say something obscene.

"Translate for us, please," the insect requested, and somehow the translation came to Nico.

"My hovercraft is full of...eels," Nico said sourly. *That's it. This is a dream.* She enjoyed Monty Python well enough, but not that much. The blue humanoid and the insect chortled more.

"Translation tag functioning. Step that way, please," the insect said.

✲

Officers waved her off two more stations after they flashed lenses at her. Nico was glad; their stations looked like medical facilities. At the second one, a man in a double-breasted pinstripe suit, wingtips, and askew fedora lay inert on the dais, having succumbed to whatever procedure he'd received. Two bald humanoids in smocks held pads and discussed data over him. Nico hurried to the last station, where a black circle lay, similar to the one in the airfield. The bored female officer standing before it gestured in its direction. She laid a three-fingered hand on Nico's shoulder to guide her.

"Don't touch me," Nico said automatically. "Um, sorry."

Nico stepped into the circle. When it flashed, Nico felt as if her underwear had been frisked.

"Hey! Mr Bear! My stuff!" she exclaimed, seeing her possessions lying in a neat row on the table, and hurried off the circle to fetch Bear.

"Can you tell us where Mr Bear comes from, please," the officer said in a bored tone, seating herself before a monitor.

"Mr Bear comes from where I came from," Nico said. "He's—"

Her thought slid away on a white surface in her mind.

"He's..." Nico frowned.

The officer glanced at something above Nico's shoulder, and when she turned to look, the floating head was staring in her direction. Nico turned back again.

"Okay, thank you," the officer said, dismissive, and Nico assumed the questioning was done.

While Nico placed Bear in his harness again, a nude man, completely hairless to his non-existent eyebrows, walked by, bypassing the search area. In his two hands he held a claymore over four feet long, the blade pointing down. Nico looked at the giant blade and then at him.

This is the most Freudian dream ever.

He moved ahead as she picked up her switchblade and put it back in her waistband. Before she pocketed her Chococat wallet, she opened it. It contained rubles, her Leningrad University student ID, a credit card, a Leningrad metro pass, and her magazine clipping of the actress Sabella Peck, dressed in a men's suit. Nico hugged the picture to her and Bear, then put her wallet away. Her passport security neck wallet had also ended up on the table; she grabbed it and the tin of breath mints she hadn't known she'd been carrying. When she glanced back at the room, wondering if it was okay to leave, the female head in the bubble coolly watched her. Nico walked quickly to where the naked man had exited.

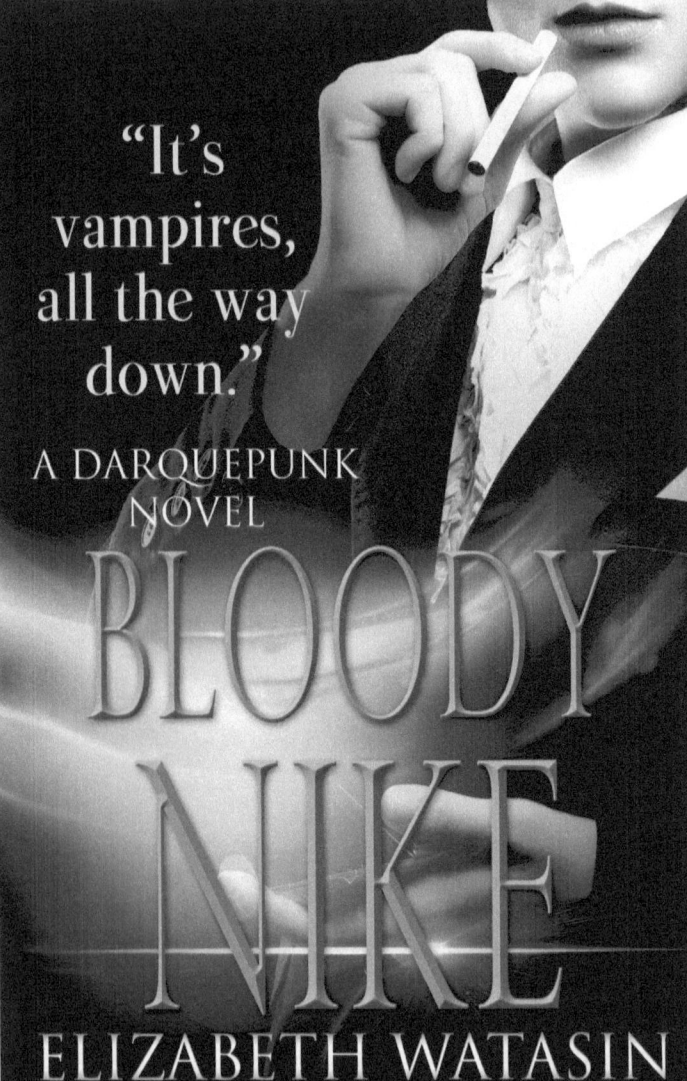

"It's
vampires,
all the way
down."

A DARQUEPUNK
NOVEL

BLOODY
NIKE

ELIZABETH WATASIN

More from Elizabeth:

The Dark Victorian: Risen Vol 1
The Dark Victorian: Bones Vol 2
Ice Demon: A Dark Victorian Penny Dread Vol 1
Medusa: A Dark Victorian Penny Dread Vol 2
Sundark: An Elle Black Penny Dread Vol 1
Poison Garden: An Elle Black Penny Dread Vol 2
Monster Stalker: A Darquepunk Novel Vol 1
Bloody Nike: A Darquepunk Novel Vol 2
Charm School Graphique Vol 1
and
Charm School Digital No 1-9

The Wrecking Faerie: A Charm School Novella Vol 1
Hot Roddin' To Hell: A Charm School Novella Vol 2

About The Author

Elizabeth Watasin is the author of the Gothic steampunk series *The Dark Victorian*, The *Elle Black Penny Dreads*, the *Darquepunk* series, and the creator/artist of the indie comics series *Charm School*. She is the winner of the 2015 Rainbow Award for Best Lesbian Fantasy and Romance Fantasy and a Gaylactic Spectrum nominee. A twenty year veteran of animation and comics, her credits include thirteen feature films, such as *Beauty and the Beast, Aladdin, The Lion King*, and *The Princess and the Frog*, and writing for *Disney Adventures* magazine. She lives in Los Angeles with her black cat named Draw, bringing readers uncanny heroines in cyberpunk, historical fantasy, diesal fantasy, and paranormal thrillers.

Sign up for the mailing list at A-Girl Studio.
www.a-girlstudio.com
amazon.com/author/elizabethwatasin
www.facebook.com/ElizabethWatasinX
twitter.com/ewatasin

ELIZABETH WATASIN

The DARK VICTORIAN

BONES

www.ingramcontent.com/pod-product-compliance
Lightning Source LLC
Chambersburg PA
CBHW030501130626
46549CB00007B/2809